PRINCESS DEATH

Tale of a Cursed Princess

Jeanne Grandilli
Shaina Rothberg

Bon Bon Books

Map Design: Alec McKinley

Printed in the United States of America

*For Peter and Mary, our beloved
parents and grandparents*

Prologue

Abaddon was abuzz with excitement. Whispers had leaked from the royal court that young Queen Citrine was at last ready to wed. Five years earlier, the twelve-year-old princess had ascended the throne under tragic circumstances after losing both parents, the beloved King and Queen, to an outbreak of the dreaded *dragon bumps*. Now that she had come of age at seventeen, frankly a little past age for those days, there was endless gossip and speculation about the young queen's love life, or lack thereof, and whom she should choose to be her future husband and king.

Citrine was a good and fair ruler, but truthfully it was her stunning beauty that caused her subjects to adore her. She was tall and slim with long, golden-blonde hair and sparkling hazel eyes that looked either green or amber brown, depending upon the light or one's eyesight

Her admiring subjects never tired of discussing Citrine's latest ball gowns and hair styles but, more than anything, they wanted their young queen to marry—or at least have a string of failed romances, which might provide their drab lives with some titillating diversion. Alas, their young queen did not seem inclined to romance—until now.

The truth was that Citrine was not in a hurry to get married. She was intelligent, capable, and independent, and not entirely convinced that she needed a king to complete her—or share her kingdom. However, she did want a family and an heir, so she had finally relented and agreed to meet some prospective suitors.

At first Queen Citrine was attracted to the very dashing and handsome young alchemist, Zimbardo. His dark good looks had caught the attention of numerous young ladies throughout the Five Kingdoms, and he was something of a celebrity, known for his daring and uncanny magical demonstrations.

Citrine was very curious to meet the attractive and accomplished young alchemist. As he bent to kiss her hand at court, she couldn't help but admire his fine, embroidered black cloak and his dazzling white smile. To all appearances, Zimbardo seemed to be the perfect suitor. He was tall, dark, and handsome, as well as clever, and claimed to own a prosperous alchemy shop. He also had his own castle, which didn't hurt.

After only two meetings with the delightfully charming alchemist, Citrine (though normally more astute) was quite smitten and agreed to marry him. Zimbardo was overjoyed upon receiving her consent to be his wife. He kissed her hands and both cheeks, as he dared not yet kiss her mouth, and passionately pledged his troth. He might have a castle, but he didn't yet have a crown. As he was quite an ambitious man, he was thrilled to think that he would soon be the King of Abaddon. Not only would he gain a wife, he would gain a throne—not to mention the great wealth of Abaddon's treasury.

With visions of Citrine and his future crown dancing in his head, Zimbardo returned to his castle to tidy up and prepare for his wedding day and coronation. However, not everyone in Citrine's court was as favorably impressed by the dashing alchemist. Three of her most trusted advisors secretly followed Zimbardo back to his castle in order to convince themselves that he was worthy of their wonderful queen. What they saw did not reassure them. Peering discreetly through the dirty castle windows, they saw large pentagrams, piles of animal skulls, and numerous books on the black arts and sorcery. As they looked on, Zimbardo chanted a diabolical incantation and threw a handful of black powder into a cauldron. Immediately, a large dark spirit rose up from the vapor and appeared to hold a pleasant conversation with him.

Having seen quite enough, the three horrified advisors fled home to tell their queen of what they had seen. Predictably, being quite infatuated, Citrine did not at first believe them. Certainly, no one wants to believe anything bad about someone who is so terribly handsome and dreamy looking.

Unwilling to believe the awful disclosure about her intended fiancé, Citrine sent two more advisors as well as her trusted young handmaid, Abigail, (who was equally smitten with Zimbardo) to go spy upon him and report back to her. They too witnessed Zimbardo conversing with dark spirits. Even Abigail had to glumly concede that he was not after all an alchemist but rather a sorcerer and practitioner of the dark arts.

Finally persuaded of Zimbardo's true nature, Citrine reluctantly sent word to him, calling off their engagement. (Secretly, Citrine was fascinated by bad boys but knew it would never do to marry one, let alone make him king.)

In those days they didn't have the internet or even telegrams, so they had to send a carrier pigeon to Zimbardo with the fateful message that his engagement to Queen Citrine was now officially cancelled inasmuch as he had falsely represented himself as a good and worthy man, while in fact being a black magician and sorcerer and all around bad guy. Upon receiving this unexpected and devastating news, Zimbardo flew into a black rage and tried to strangle the poor bird for being the bearer of such bad tidings. The pigeon fought back by bombing the irate sorcerer with a barrage of *droppings,* which landed on the front of his fancy silk jacket.

Distracted, he released the pigeon, which managed to flap safely away minus only a few tail feathers.

Zimbardo went on to throw a monumental temper tantrum, breaking almost everything in his castle and causing even the dark spirits to shrink away from him in fear. He was furious at being jilted by Citrine. After all, where else was he going to find such a sweet deal: a beautiful queen, a kingship, *and* a wealthy kingdom? He reviewed his other prospects, but unfortunately they were not very promising. Most of the other kingdoms had aging, married queens or were too shabby for his lofty, status-seeking taste. Exhausted by all the destruction, Zimbardo finally collected himself and began to plot his revenge.

Meanwhile, back in Abaddon, a disappointed Queen Citrine continued to meet with other suitors. Unfortunately, none of them were as handsome and charming as the rakish Zimbardo. She feared she might have to settle for an ugly, boring man until the afternoon that Prince Azrael walked into court. Azrael was tall and good-looking and proved to be a witty and intelligent conversationalist. As the youngest son of neighboring royalty, he had his own modest fortune and was a natural scholar. In short, he was just about perfect, and Queen Citrine fell madly in love with him, forgetting all about the deceitful, if charming, Zimbardo. Unfortunately, he had not forgotten her.

The wedding day of Queen Citrine and Prince Azrael dawned a bit gray and gloomy. However, as the hour of their wedding approached, the clouds disappeared, and the sun shone down in its full brilliance, as though to give a blessing to the happy couple. Citrine looked truly resplendent as she walked down the aisle in her flowing white wedding gown, while Azrael had never looked more handsome than in his royal dress uniform. The wedding took place in Abaddon's royal chapel. Roses, lilies and jasmine were draped everywhere so that the entire chapel was sweetly perfumed with their delicate scents.

The blissful couple had just been joined in marriage and enjoyed their first kiss when the light suddenly dimmed and black smoke began to fill the chapel. A moment later, everyone gasped as Zimbardo stepped out of the smoke, clutching a magnificent bouquet of blood red roses.

"So sorry to interrupt the festivities. I just wanted to drop by, pay my disrespect, and give you kids a little wedding gift." He approached Citrine,

presenting her with the beautiful bouquet of dark red roses.
"Congratulations on your marriage. Unfortunately, because you chose to
betray me, Citrine, you will not live happily ever after. I curse your
firstborn child with *the touch of death*." Ominously, he sprinkled some
black powder upon the bouquet, causing it to immediately shrivel and die.
One by one, the blackened petals floated to the ground. Smirking, Zimbardo
gave a small bow and then vanished along with the smoke.

Citrine shrieked and fainted away while pandemonium erupted in the
chapel. The panicked guests fled, shouting and screaming for their lives.
Distraught, Azrael caught his new bride in his arms. Slowly, she opened
her eyes and looked up him, dazed and stunned, but otherwise unhurt. "I'm
frightened, Azrael. What if the curse comes true?"

Azrael tried bravely to reassure Citrine that he would allow no harm
to come to her or any future child, though secretly he too greatly feared the
curse of the evil sorcerer.

Tragically, it seemed that the queen had indeed been cursed, as she
died the following year after giving birth to a beautiful baby daughter. With
her dying breath, she cradled the child in her arms and whispered to her
husband, "*She has eyes of. . . indigo.*"

Sadly, those were the young queen's last words. King Azrael was
heartbroken, but honored his wife by naming their daughter *Indigo*.
Although she looked like a normal child, the king soon realized that
something was not right with the young princess. She was seldom seen
outside of the castle, and rumor spread throughout the Five Kingdoms that
Princess Indigo had been cursed.

Chapter One

Princess Indigo

Princess Indigo had finally come of age and her father, King Azrael, had decided to throw a grand debut ball and invite all of the eligible young men in the Five Kingdoms. Frantic preparations were underway in preparation for the gala event. In the grand ballroom the servants were busy polishing everything to a high shine and laying out all of the finest royal china and silver. A profusion of flower displays from the extensive castle gardens provided a splash of color and lent an air of festivity. The long buffet tables were crowded with silver platters heaped high with the most exquisite delicacies, and fine wines had been decanted into crystal and silver pitchers. In short, it was a feast fit for a king—or a mystery princess in need of suitors.

King Azrael, still a handsome and elegant man, if now a bit grey at the temples, strode anxiously through the ballroom, checking on the preparations. He caught sight of Abigail, Citrine's former handmaid, as she hurried in from the kitchen bearing a brimming silver punch bowl, which threatened to slosh over at the slightest wobble. With a great sigh of relief, the maid carefully placed the heavy bowl in the center of a buffet table. Discreetly, she dipped a ladle into the frothing punch and sampled the potent brew, hoping to calm her nerves a bit. Abigail had put on a bit of weight since her youth and had matured into a stern, if soft hearted, matron, who was not to be trifled with.

The maid jumped guiltily as King Azrael appeared suddenly at the buffet table. Gulping down the last of the punch, she pretended to busy herself polishing the ladle.

"Abigail, is the princess almost ready? The guests will be arriving shortly."

The maid's eyes flew wide. She'd been so busy overseeing the food preparations she truly had no idea of the princess's current whereabouts. "Yes, sir, I'll see to her. I'm sure she's almost ready." She knew the king was already anxious and did not want to add to his concerns.

"Please make sure she's on her best behavior tonight," he implored her. "It's important that she make a good impression."

"I'll do my best, sir, but you know the princess has a mind of her own..." she reminded him. In public, maid and king kept up a formal distance, though in private they were more like family.

She poured the king a cup of the punch, which he quaffed down with approval. "Very nice...that should help to keep everyone happy."

Abigail smiled and nodded appreciatively at him. "Well, I'd better see to the princess.

"Please do, " urged the king.

Abigail curtsied to the king and hurried off to find her royal charge.

With a sigh, King Azrael strode off to continue his oversight of the final details for the evening. He was checking everything twice to insure that all would go smoothly. Even so, he could not quell a lingering sense of unease, which the punch had done little to abate. Indigo had expressed absolutely no interest in marriage, but he was getting older and, as a single parent, he worried about leaving her alone with an unsettled future. He was, therefore, determined to find her a suitable husband as soon as possible. However, because of all the unfortunate rumors circulating about the young princess, he knew this might be a difficult task. As Indigo seldom ventured out of the castle, few people had even seen her. The rumors were grossly exaggerated, though it was true, she did have a small problem…

By hosting the ball, the king hoped to dispel the rumors and at least introduce Princess Indigo to society. They would see for themselves that the worst rumors were untrue and that she was not, as rumored, *an ugly witch who could kill you with just one look.* Far from it, she had been a sweet, sensitive, and loving child, who would never deliberately harm anyone.

In truth, Princess Indigo appeared to be a perfectly normal, lovely young girl, but, as we all know, appearances can be deceiving. She had a slim, lithe figure and was of average height. In the sunlight, her long, flowing dark hair shone with flecks of both gold and copper. But it was her large remarkable eyes, which would most impress you. They were an unusual and exquisite shade of deep purple blue. As her mother had noted, they were exactly the color of indigo, which is one of the most heavenly colors.

The second thing you would likely notice about the young princess was that her hands were always covered by gleaming sterling silver gauntlets. These were like hand armor, but because they were fashioned by the finest craftsman, they were neither heavy nor bulky. They were constructed of a fine silver mesh, which allowed for complete flexibility of her fingers. As they were decorated with beautiful gemstones, they were truly like works of art. The young princess was never seen without them. Naturally, everyone was curious about these gauntlets, and there were many rumors about them. Some said that the young princess simply enjoyed wearing them. (If you had sparkly, gem-studded silver gauntlets, you would probably want to wear them too.)

However, others at the court imagined a darker reason for the gauntlets. They said that it was part of her curse and that under the gauntlets she had sharp claws like those of a wild animal. Others said that if she touched you with her bare hand, you would surely die. As you might imagine, Indigo didn't have a lot of friends. For the most part, her devoted father, King Azrael, had raised her alone in the castle, though she was also very close to Abigail, who had been her primary attendant since her birth.

Despite her lack of friends, Indigo was not at all lonely. She was a bright, inquisitive girl who enjoyed spending time alone in the large glass greenhouse that had belonged to her mother. Citrine had been an herbalist and healer, and it seemed that Indigo had inherited her mother's talent, as well as her laboratory inside the greenhouse, which Indigo had greatly expanded for the purpose of her own research. The shimmering glass greenhouse was full of exotic trees, colorful flowers, and all manner of medicinal herbs. The high ceiling of the greenhouse sparkled with crystals of all colors, and the bookshelves were lined with antique volumes on botany and biology. At one end of the greenhouse, there was even a small pond full of frogs and pink lotus flowers.

In the far corner of the greenhouse, you might also notice a large round bed embroidered on the side with the letters "N-Y-X." This belonged to the large and magnificent silver wolf, Nyx, who was Indigo's constant companion and guardian. Nyx had piercing blue eyes, almost as deep as Indigo's and bore a small crescent moon etched on the back of his left ear. The silver wolf had been with Indigo since she was a small child and had discovered the wolf cub in the nearby forest with its paw caught in a bear trap. Despite her father's fears that the wolf might harm her, she had insisted upon taking him home and nursing the pup back to health. Since then, the silver wolf had been utterly devoted to the young princess and seldom left her side. He was fiercely protective of her, as well as keenly intelligent.

Abigail flew up the grand staircase in search of her missing charge. Out of breath, she hurried into Indigo's bedchamber. The spacious room was definitely fit for a princess with its ivory and gilt-edged paneling and long golden draperies. Everything was in its place—except for the princess. She knocked on the closed door of the bath chamber. "Indigo, are you in there?" Getting no answer, she opened the door and poked her head inside the chamber, which held a large, claw-footed tub surrounded by beautiful blue and white tiles—but no sign of the princess.

Abigail bustled back into the bedchamber and got down on her hands and knees to look under the large canopied bed. No Indigo. She began opening the closet doors that took up one side of the room. "I know you don't want to go to the ball tonight, but you're not going to get out of it this time." She opened the last closet, which was full of lavish ball gowns. On

9

one shelf, there stood a half dozen small hand forms, bearing an assortment of the princess's beautiful, gem-studded silver gauntlets. Shaking her head, Abigail exited the room and ran back down the staircase. She kept running all the way through the busy castle kitchen, grabbed a cloak from the hook near the door, and dashed outside.

* * *

Instead of getting ready for the ball, Indigo was in her greenhouse, conducting another experiment, although you would hardly know it was her under the long white coat and large protective goggles she wore. Holding a beaker full of bubbling liquid, she carefully poured in a mysterious ingredient.

As usual, Nyx sat at her feet, warily eyeing the proceedings.

"Okay, Nyx, I need some mandrake, self-help, blood root, and a sprinkle of crushed red crystal," ordered Indigo.

Obediently, Nyx trotted over to the shelves and retrieved the requested ingredients. One by one, Indigo poured the items into her bubbling beaker. She sniffed it, wrinkling her nose. Screwing her eyes shut, she lifted the beaker to her lips and gulped down the entire contents, trying not to gag on the bitter potion. Carefully, she removed one of her silver gauntlets, revealing a discolored hand and blackened fingernails. Cautiously, she laid a bared finger on a small green plant lying on the table. Instantly, the plant shriveled up and died.

"Blast! Another failure! I'll make the next one stronger." She took up a notebook itemizing a long list of ingredients. Using a quill, she checked off the last ones used.

"All right, Nyx," she said, sighing. "Let's try Lady's Mantle, half a squill, a dose of wormwood, hydrochloric acid, and essence of agrimony."

Nyx returned to the shelves to retrieve the new ingredients. One by one, Indigo poured them into the beaker. She turned back to Nyx, "Oh, and a pinch of powdered dragon's tongue."

Nyx cocked his head at her as if to say *really?* But he retrieved the vial of dragon's tongue, holding it carefully in his teeth, and reluctantly gave it to his mistress.

"This should give it a nice kick," Indigo nodded with satisfaction.

No fool, Nyx retreated to the corner, closed his eyes, and put his paws over his ears.

Carefully, Indigo dropped a pinch of the dragon's tongue into the beaker. Immediately, the contents begin to bubble ferociously. Smoke billowed up followed by a loud explosion.

At that untimely moment, Abigail burst into the greenhouse, just in time to see Indigo swallowed up by a cloud of smoke.

Growling softly, Nyx slunk toward Abigail.

"Oh hush, Nyx! It's just me." She turned her attention to Indigo. "I knew I'd find you in here."

Coughing, Indigo stepped out of the smoke. "Oh, hey, Abigail," she said casually. "What brings you here?"

"Don't give me that," Abigail said sternly.

"I'm not going!" exclaimed Indigo. Defiantly, she turned away from her maid, revealing that the back of her hair was in flames!

"Oh lord, your hair's on fire!" shouted Abigail.

Peering over her shoulder at her flaming hair, Indigo shrieked and jumped into the nearby small pond. A moment later, she emerged, dripping and smoldering, with a small green frog on her head.

"I can't possibly go to the ball looking like this!" Indigo protested. "Besides, I'm making progress on my cure."

"By blowing yourself up?" snorted Abigail. She wrapped a sturdy arm around her charge and propelled her toward the door. "Come along now. No more excuses. Somehow, I've got to make you look like a princess," she grumbled.

Nyx jumped to his feet, prepared to follow his mistress out of the greenhouse. "Sorry, Nyx. You're not invited. We can't have you scaring the guests," said Abigail, shaking her head at the disappointed wolf.

"Don't worry, Nyx, I'll bring you a treat later," Indigo promised, patting the large wolf on his nose. "Anyway, you're lucky you don't have to go to the stupid ball. I wish I could stay here, too."

Unconvinced, Nyx grumbled and retreated to his plush wolf bed where he curled up inside and went to sleep.

It was already twilight as Abigail and Indigo trudged up the long path from the greenhouse back to the castle. In preparation for the grand ball, the castle was lit up by great candle filled sconces and gleamed

11

magnificently in the gathering night.   So as not to be seen, the two slipped into the castle through the kitchen, which was bustling with activity and full of very mouthwatering aromas. The kitchen staff looked quite surprised to see a wet and sooty-looking Indigo with a frog on her head.

"Mind your business. There's plenty more work to do," Abigail snapped at the gawking staff as she hurried the princess through the kitchen.

The chef stepped forward eagerly, staring at Indigo's head. "Please, may I have the frog?"

Surprised, the princess cupped a hand to her head, causing the small frog to leap off her head and hop urgently away before the disappointed chef could pop him into his stewpot.

Before leaving the kitchen, Abigail snatched up a white tablecloth and draped it over Indigo's head. "We can't risk your father seeing you like this or he might have a coronary," scolded the maid.

They made it half way up the grand staircase before King Azrael spotted them on his way down. "Please tell me that isn't Indigo under that cloth," groaned the king.

"I'm not Indigo, I'm a ghost," Indigo said in low, muffled tones from under the tablecloth.

"I don't even want to know," the king sighed. "Just see that she's ready in half an hour."

"Yes, Your Majesty, don't worry.   She'll be ready," Abigail reassured the worried king as she hurried Indigo up the stairs and into her bedchamber.

Shaking his head in dismay, the king continued downstairs to his library where he poured himself a full glass of sherry.

In her bath chamber, Indigo submerged herself in a large tub full of bubbles. Playfully, she molded a bubble beard and moustache for herself. She thought she would take a nice long bath and dawdle as much as possible. She absolutely, positively did not want to attend this ball. It was unfair of her father to force her. After all, she never forced him to do anything.   She did not care if she ever made her debut into society, and she did not even want to think about getting married.

She felt anxious and sick to her stomach at the very thought of having a husband. For you see, some of those rumors that were circulating about the princess were unfortunately true. Indigo had indeed been cursed by the sorcerer's evil spell. She must always wear the silver gauntlets because if she touched any living thing...or anyone...with her bare hand it *would* surely die. She couldn't risk getting too close to anyone. That's why she seldom ventured outside of the castle, and why she paid no calls on her neighbors.

What if she were to get married and then accidentally touch her husband with her bare hand? Or what if *he* forgot and touched her hands? He would die a horrible death, and she—and probably her father—would be arrested and executed on charges of murder and witchcraft. That's why she had shut herself up in the castle and why she spent so much time alone in her greenhouse. She was trying desperately to create a cure for her deadly curse so that nothing and no one would ever come to any harm by her hand...accidentally or otherwise...

Abigail bustled in just then holding a large pitcher of water. "All right, stop playing around. We need to get you dressed." She poured the pitcher of water over Indigo's soapy head. Sputtering, she rose reluctantly from the tub, and Abigail handed her a large towel monogrammed with the letter *A* (for Abaddon). Once she was wrapped in the towel, the maid handed her a dry pair of the silver gauntlets, which were embedded with a row of blue sapphires. "These will go well with your gown."

After Indigo pulled on the gleaming gauntlets, Abigail pushed her behind the tall dressing screen, which had once belonged to her mother. The beautiful screen was covered with porcelain ivory edged in gilt and decorated with a delicate floral scene. One by one, the maid handed the young princess numerous items of clothing, including several pieces of underwear, a corset, several very *poufy* slips and finally a gorgeous ball gown and high-heeled slippers made of indigo blue to match her eyes.

"All right, that's everything. Come out and let me look at you," commanded Abigail. There was a long silent pause behind the screen. "Well, what are you waiting for?" the maid asked impatiently.

"I'm not ready," protested Indigo.

"Come out anyway," demanded Abigail. "I'll be the judge of that."

Uncertainly, Indigo stepped out from behind the porcelain screen. If you only looked at her from the neck down, she was a perfect vision of satiny indigo blue. Unfortunately, from the neck up, she looked a perfect fright. Her long dark hair was singed from the flames and the short ends stood up in all directions.

"Oh dear!" exclaimed Abigail in dismay. "You can't go out looking like that."

"I told you I wasn't ready," Indigo said a bit petulantly.

"Come, sit down and let's fix you up…as best we can," Abigail heaved a heavy sigh as Indigo sat down at her vanity table, staring glumly into the mirror at the fried ends of her once beautiful, long hair.

"Good luck," said the reluctant princess, rolling her eyes.

Abigail took a step back, studying Indigo's singed tresses. "Now, what are we going to do about that hair?"

"If you can't fix it, I guess I can't go," offered Indigo hopefully.

"Nonsense!" said the no nonsense maid. "We'll just make a few little snips." Quickly, she snipped off the singed ends. "Then we'll just tuck it up and pin it into a nice tidy bun." Indigo's hair now actually looked quite becoming and showed no signs of fire damage. Next, Abigail deftly applied small touches of makeup, which was all the young princess really needed, including some dark blue powder to outline her eyes and bring out their deep indigo color.

As a final touch, she slipped a gorgeous diamond and sapphire tiara over her head. "There," she nodded with satisfaction. "Now you look like a princess!"

Indigo stared at herself in the vanity mirror, hardly recognizing her own image. Abigail was right. For the first time in her life, Indigo thought she did look rather like a princess. And she rather liked it.

There was a soft knock at the door, which pushed open slightly. "May I come in?" called King Azrael. "Yes, father…I'm ready…I think." Indigo turned away from her mirror and rose to greet her father as he entered the room.

As he caught sight of his daughter, the king froze in his tracks. Never had he seen her look like anything other than a gawky, awkward child. Now she stood before him transformed into an extraordinarily lovely young woman. He had no idea Indigo could ever look like that. Maybe finding her a husband wouldn't be so difficult after all he thought.

"Indigo, you look beautiful," the king beamed. He sniffed the air with a frown, "Is something burning?"

14

Indigo and Abigail looked at each other and shrugged innocently. With her foot, Abigail discreetly kicked away the singed ends of Indigo's hair still lying on the floor.

King Azrael slipped a hand inside his jacket pocket and withdrew a small blue velvet box. "Tonight is a very important night, Indigo. Every eligible prince from the Five Kingdoms will be here."

"But father," protested Indigo. "I'm not ready for a relationship. I kill things. Remember?"

King Azrael heaved a heavy sigh. "How could I forget? I won't pretend I'm not concerned, but as long as you keep your gauntlets on, all should go well." He held out the velvet box to her. "I brought you something for good luck."

Indigo took the box from her father and opened it. Inside the box was a most exquisite pair of sparkling earrings, which seemed to contain all the colors of the rainbow. "Oh father, they're amazing!" gasped Indigo.

"They belonged to your mother. I've been waiting for a special occasion to give them to you. Just think, you could meet your future husband tonight," the king remarked hopefully.

Indigo immediately tried on the earrings. They looked stunning on her and perfectly complimented her gown. "Oh, I love them! Thank you, father. I'll treasure them forever," she exclaimed breathlessly. The king smiled with pleasure.

"But I still don't want to get married," she added.

The king's face fell. "Indigo, I'm getting old and I want to see you happily settled before I die."

"Oh, Father, you're not dying. And I'm not ready to be married!" she exclaimed in exasperation.

The king sighed. "You will be when you find the right man. But you won't find him if you don't look."

Resigned, Indigo shook her head. "Fine. Let's get this over with."

King Azrael held out his arm to her. "Come along, there's a ballroom full of young men dying to meet you."

Playfully, Indigo lunged at her father, waving her hands in mock menace.

The king chuckled, ruefully. "You know what I meant." Firmly, he took Indigo's arm under his own and escorted her out of the room.

Jeanne Grandilli and Shaina Rothberg

Chapter Two

The Ill-fated Ball

Over at Beringer Palace, the seven princes of Beringer were equally reluctant to attend Princess Indigo's debut ball.   In descending order, the eldest son was named Boron, the second Neon, the third Argon, the fourth Zenon, the fifth Radon, the sixth Barium, and the youngest, Ion.   Beringer was not quite as prosperous a kingdom as Abaddon, and the crown would, of course, pass only to the eldest heir, Boron. Therefore, The King of Beringer was hopeful that one of his younger sons might find the favor of young Princess Indigo and, thereby, join the great kingdoms of Beringer and Abaddon. However, he knew this was wishful thinking as none of his sons had expressed the least bit of interest in meeting the princess and were only attending the ball on pain of disinheritance.

If the king were honest, he was also aware that none of his sons was exactly a *catch* for the young Princess of Abaddon.   Alas, most of them had taken after him and had the Beringer nose, which was rather large and not very attractive. However, his youngest son, Ion, had the good fortune to take after his mother, the queen, who had quite a nice nose. Therefore, he was, by far the best looking of his sons.   Unfortunately, Ion was also rather wild and unpredictable and didn't show the least inclination to settle down or find a wife.　　　　"Oh well," sighed the king. He too had heard the dark rumors about the young princess and could not entirely blame his sons for being reluctant to make her acquaintance. Hopefully, they would all return home safe and sound and still in one piece.

Up in the princes' chamber, there was much grumbling among the brothers as they finished dressing for the ball. "Just because I'm the oldest doesn't mean I should have to marry her," declared Boron, as he pulled up his stockings. "Besides, I'll inherit father's crown one day, so I don't really have to worry. I'm set. But one of you really should marry her. After all, you could one day be the King of Abaddon, which is quite a grand kingdom." He turned expectantly to Neon, the second eldest.

"Don't look at me. I don't want any part of her!" Neon declared hotly. "Besides, you know they say she's a witch. I don't want to be killed in my sleep."

Father knows I'm in love with Princess Clarissa, so why should I have to go?" asked Argon.

"Because Princess Clarissa doesn't know you're alive," said Neon, not very nicely.

"I still don't want to go," he said, emphatically. "I'd rather remain a bachelor for the rest of my life than marry a cursed witch, who's probably ugly to boot."

"If you don't go, "I'm not going either," said Zenon.

"Come on," piped up Radon. "How bad can she be?"

"I hear she can kill you with just one look," said Barium.

"Maybe we can send word that we have the plague," offered Boron.

The princes pondered this suggestion.

Neon glanced suddenly around the crowded chamber. "Hey, where's Ion?"

Realizing their youngest brother was missing, the princes jumped up to find him, but it was too late.

Prince Ion was already crouched upon the windowsill and, as his brothers ran toward him, shouting in protest, he leapt from the open window, hoping to land upon the back of his black stallion, Lucifer, who was waiting below. Unfortunately, the horse was spooked by all the shouting and commotion and ran off, causing Ion to make a hard landing in the bushes below.   Wincing a bit, he got to his feet and dusted himself off.

From above him, his brothers leaned out of the chamber window, calling him every nasty name they could think of. "Come back here, you coward!" shouted Boron.

"I'm telling father," said Argon. "He'll disinherit you."

"Fine with me," shrugged Ion. "I'm not getting anything anyway."

"Take me with you," pleaded Zenon.

"Sorry, bro, no can do," said Ion.

"That's not fair," pouted Barium.

"Good luck with *Princess Death*," Ion grinned and waved to his brothers before he turned and limped off into the woods to find his horse. Unfortunately, Lucifer, his not so trusty steed, had disappeared, so he was forced to walk on foot through the forest. Truthfully, he didn't really mind walking. It was a beautiful day, and he was just happy to have escaped the palace—not to mention the ball at Abaddon.

Princess Indigo was probably some kind of secret monster. He didn't care how rich her father was; when he married it would be only for love and that of course wouldn't be for a very long time.   He had noticed that there were quite a few fetching young ladies throughout the Five Kingdoms, and he planned to get to know all of them, one by one.   After all, he was young and in no hurry to marry.

Because Ion was quite tall and handsome with a head of dusty blonde hair and big green eyes, the ladies were equally eager to meet him. However, apart from his excellent looks, he didn't have much else to offer. As the youngest of seven sons, he would never become king unless the plague claimed all six of his brothers (or they all killed each other in a royal power struggle). As it was highly unlikely that he would ever ascend to the throne of Beringer, Ion could count on little, if any, inheritance from his father.

Thus, it was important that Ion learn a trade that might earn him a good income and a secure future. He had already tried several professions with no luck.   He had tried banking but found he kept reversing his numbers (before anyone knew about dyslexia).   He tried being a baker but found he would rather eat bread than bake it. He tried being a blacksmith but kept burning his fingers. He thought about becoming a preacher, but quickly dismissed that idea as it would unfortunately require him to model good behavior at all times.

Currently, he was apprenticed to a renowned wizard named Zozimo, an accomplished herbalist and healer, who ran a thriving apothecary shop in the woods. Ion was intrigued by the wizard's uncanny skill and hoped to learn a great deal from him. Besides, he liked the satisfaction of mixing up potions that could help people.

It was almost dusk when Ion arrived at the small shop in the woods. A crooked sign over the shop door announced *Zozimo's Potions.* A long line of ailing villagers stretched out of the doorway, waiting for a healing potion from the astute wizard.

As Ion attempted to make his way to the entrance, he was elbowed aside by an annoyed older gentleman, "Hey, where do you think you're going? Wait your turn like everyone else," he pointed to the rear of the long line.

"Sorry, I work here," said Ion.

"Leave 'em be. I recognize the lad," said the old woman behind him. "He's Zozimo's assistant." She turned to Ion, "Hurry up, lad. I swear he's getting slower every day."

Ion nodded his thanks to the woman and hurried through the door. Inside, the small shop was dim and chock full of ancient books, vials of potions, bizarre looking things floating in jars, obscure wall maps, and a skeleton or two. Colorful crystals hung from the rafters and there were several crystal balls of various sizes.

Zozimo stood behind the worn wooden counter, waiting on customers. He was an older, balding man clad in a baggy brown robe covered over by an orange apron imprinted with the shop logo, *Zozimo's Potions.* As he was not at all impressive looking, and his manner was vague and absentminded, it was easy to underestimate him or think him a fool. In truth, he was the wisest wizard in all of the Five Kingdoms. Nothing escaped his notice except perhaps his glasses, which he was constantly misplacing.

Assisting Zozimo at the counter was his unlikely companion and helper, Bijou, a large, very intelligent black bat, who appeared to understand everything. Like his master, he also wore an orange apron with the shop logo, though of course it was a good deal smaller. The orange shop apron caused the bat's yellow-orange eyes to glow like two shining jack-o'-lanterns.

Zozimo looked surprised to see Ion as he dashed into the shop. "Ion, I wasn't expecting you today. Weren't you going to the ball at Abaddon?"

Ion shrugged innocently as he tied on his own orange, *logoed* apron. "I...uh...changed my mind."

"Oh well," said the wizard. "I'm glad you're here. It's getting late, and we still have all these orders to fill." He grabbed up the next order and squinted at it. "Blast it all! Where are my glasses?"

Bijou pointed a wing toward his head. Taking the hint, Zozimo retrieved his glasses from the top of his head and pushed them to the end of his nose.

Ion dutifully took his place behind the counter next to Zozimo and Bijou. "Next!" he called. A heavyset, ugly woman approached Ion at the counter. "Yes, madam, how can I help you today?"

"I need a love potion...extra strong...and this one had better work. I want men to find me irresistible," demanded the ugly woman.

Ion couldn't help staring at the large wart on the tip of the woman's nose. "Perhaps I could recommend some wart remover?" he ventured uncertainly.

"Are you implying that I have warts?" the woman huffed, greatly insulted.

Ion immediately backed off apologetically. "Of course not, madam. I just thought perhaps you might want it for a...friend...who might have warts."

"I don't want wart remover!" the woman exclaimed, raising her voice. "I want a love potion!"

Ion furrowed his brow, thinking hard. "All right, madam...I'm always up for a challenge. I'll be right back." He hurried off into the cluttered back room of the shop, which served as both a storeroom and laboratory. The crowded shelves were crammed full of half-done potions, strange charms, old books and papers. On a lower shelf you might also notice two small hand forms with an unfinished pair of familiar looking silver gauntlets. Ion did not notice the gauntlets, as he was too busy trying to find a super strength love potion for the ugly woman, which, as you might imagine, was no easy task.

Finally, his eyes lighted upon a large whiskey bottle, which was probably Zozimo's private stock. No matter, he grabbed up the bottle and plastered a large label, reading *Zozimo's Potions* over the whiskey label. "That should do it," he muttered to himself.

Ion returned to the shop counter and presented the disguised whiskey bottle to the ugly woman. "There you are, madam, a surefire love potion. Just make sure that the gentleman finishes the bottle, and he'll believe that you are the most beautiful woman alive," he assured her with his most charming smile.

"Well, it's about time," the woman snapped, grabbing the bottle from him. "You'd better hope this works or I'll be back."

"No need for that, I'm sure," he smiled.

The ugly woman tossed him a few coins, and dashed out of the shop, clutching the *love potion* to her chest.

Shaking his head, Ion turned back to the counter. "Next," he called.

* * *

Back at Abaddon Castle, the ballroom was milling with royal, well-dressed guests, though King Azrael and Princess Indigo had yet to make their appearance. The orchestra was playing some lively tunes of the day, but no one was as yet on the dance floor. For the most part, the curious and evidently hungry guests were clustered in small, gossiping groups around the lavishly laid out buffet tables. Mounds of food quickly disappeared from the large silver platters but were just as quickly replenished, especially the desserts, which included the most delectable little cakes and tarts.

King Azrael had spared no expense in entertaining his guests and hoped to impress them with his hospitality and generosity. After all, there hadn't been a royal ball at Abaddon since before Citrine had died. For many years, he had been too sad to bother entertaining his neighbors. Certainly, many women had tried, over the years, to catch the eye of the handsome widower king, but unfortunately no one could come close to Citrine, and he would not settle for less. However, now that Indigo was of age, he had decided that it was necessary for both of them to re-enter society. Still, he secretly worried that the ball might be a mistake. Indigo had told him repeatedly that she wasn't ready for marriage, but he had forced the issue.   Now he had to admit to some misgivings and a nervous feeling in the pit of his stomach. However, he reasoned that as long as she wore the protective silver gauntlets and touched nothing and no one with her bare hands, there should be no problem.

Basically, the king regarded his daughter's curse as a handicap, an unfortunate impediment but not fatal—at least not to her. It was just something that she had to accept and learn to live with—indefinitely, if not forever. He knew she was trying to find a cure to heal herself, but he feared it was all a fruitless waste of time as there was likely no cure to be found. He tried to reassure himself that she would be fine and that all would go well tonight at the ball.   Nonetheless, he planned to keep a very close eye on her just in case...

These thoughts were running anxiously through the king's mind as he escorted Indigo to the top of the grand staircase prior to making their official entrance onto the ballroom floor below.   He patted her arm and gave her a reassuring smile as they braced themselves to become the center of everyone's attention.

The Royal Herald read their names, announcing them to the court. "His Highness, King Azrael, and Princess Indigo of Abaddon."

Taking a deep breath, Indigo clutched her father's arm tightly and began her long, seemingly endless descent down the gleaming spiral staircase.   As they walked, a hush fell over the ballroom.   Gazing down, Indigo saw a sea of upturned faces, gawking at her with unabashed curiosity —and outright suspicion.   She could see the whispering behind the fans. Fortunately, she could not hear them.

Down on the dance floor, an older woman whispered to her friend, "She's a beauty all right, like her mother, but don't get too close or she'll kill you."

Her friend nodded, knowingly. "They say she's a sorceress with an evil eye."   The two of them waited fearfully as Indigo made her way toward them.

A long line of suitors had already formed on the ballroom floor, dutifully waiting their turn to be introduced to the princess. All of them looked scared, including the six princes of Beringer, who appeared terribly nervous and ill at ease. One by one, the Royal Herald announced each suitor to the princess. After his name was called, each suitor inched forward a few steps (keeping a notably long distance from the princess), bowed briefly, and then nervously scuttled away.

Indigo tried to smile and nod graciously at each fleeing suitor, but she was so embarrassed that it was all she could do to keep from fleeing herself.

After the last suitor had been announced and rapidly departed, the princess found herself left standing awkwardly alone in the middle of the ballroom.

Seeing her dilemma, King Azrael cued the Royal Orchestra Conductor who immediately struck up a lively waltz tune. Swiftly, the king crossed to Indigo's side and took hold of her silver clad hands. Gracefully, he began to whirl her around the dance floor. Somewhat reassured, other dancers ventured onto the floor, making sure to keep a healthy distance from the waltzing king and princess…just in case…

Indigo whispered to her father as they danced. "I knew this would happen. Everyone is afraid of me."

"Just keep smiling and look everyone in the eye," encouraged the king.

Obeying her father, Indigo smiled brightly and began to stare at nearby dancers as they whirled by. Fearing sudden death, the stared-at-dancers abruptly whirled away from Indigo's *eye-lock*.

Sighing, Indigo turned back to the king. "It's no use, father. They think I have the Evil Eye."

"Nonsense!" he exclaimed. "Just keep smiling and dancing, but… uh…perhaps it's better not to stare at anyone. Trust me, they're going to love you."

Indigo looked askance at her father. He must be kidding. Obviously, everyone there hated her and was doing their best to avoid her.

Deliberately, King Azrael steered Indigo toward Prince Boron as he danced by with a tall redhead. The king tapped Boron on the shoulder, abruptly handed off Indigo to him, and then quickly danced off with the redhead.

Seeing the unexpected exchange, a dramatic hush fell over the ballroom. Uncertainly, Princess Indigo lifted her silver clad hands to Prince Boron, who stood frozen in fear before her. Gathering his courage, he slowly raised his hands to hers.

The entire ballroom gasped as Indigo gently took hold of the prince's hands with her silver gauntlets.

Seeing that he had not disintegrated, Prince Boron relaxed somewhat, and they slowly began to dance. The other dancers looked reassured, as well, and began to dance a bit closer to the now smoothly waltzing pair. Gaining courage, Boron smiled boldly at Indigo and now began to show off by whirling her rapidly around the ballroom.

Still dancing with the tall redhead, King Azrael smiled and nodded to his daughter as she danced by, a bit dizzily, with the rapidly whirling prince.

Emboldened by Boron's success, Prince Irwin of Vulgaria, who was quite short, tapped Boron on the shoulder and exchanged his petite brunette partner for Princess Indigo, who towered above him.

Seeing the exchange, King Azrael smiled encouragingly at his daughter. After thanking the redhead for the dance, the king left her at the side of the dance floor and moved off to address two Palace Guards. "Keep a close eye on the princess and make sure that she doesn't get into any trouble."

The guards nodded and moved off to observe the princess at a discreet distance.

Indigo was now dancing with the awkward and ungainly Prince Derrick of Lagostan, who had already stepped on her feet twice. Ineptly, he backed her into another couple, who lost their footing and took a tumble.

While Prince Derrick apologized profusely and helped the fallen dancers to their feet, Indigo took the opportunity to escape the clumsy prince and hurried over to the punch bowl.

As she stood, sipping punch, Indigo scanned the ballroom. So far, none of the princes had impressed her in the least. Certainly, none of them was husband material. Oh well, perhaps she had overlooked someone. As she thought this, Prince Carrick of Gurney approached her. At first sight, he appeared tall and rather good-looking, if a bit stiff. Her hopes rose a bit.

"I understand that you're interested in gardening, Princess Indigo."

She nodded, smiling at him. Perhaps she would finally have an interesting conversation.

"Sheep fertilizer is sadly underestimated by most serious gardeners, don't you think, Princess Indigo?" he asked very earnestly.

Indigo blinked at him already bored and mentally crossed Prince Carrick off her list of potential suitors. "Let me check on that and get back to you," she smiled sweetly at him and quickly moved off.

Feeling a bit hungry, Indigo retreated to the buffet table and began loading up her plate with her favorite foods, including crispy chicken bits and noodles smothered in golden cheese. She had a mouthful of chicken, when the rotund Prince Barium approached her.

"Oh yum," he said, peering at her plate. "Chicken bits are my favorite. Do you mind?"

She was just offering him her plate when he reached clumsily for a chicken bit, and instead managed to knock off one of her mother's sparkling earrings.

As she watched in horror, the earring rolled away onto the dance floor. Just as she bent over to retrieve the earring, it was accidentally kicked away by a passing dancer. Alarmed, Indigo chased after her rolling earring. She was just about to snatch it up, when it was kicked away once more by another dancer, who was quite large. This time, the earring sailed off the dance floor through the open doors leading out to the veranda.

In a panic to save her mother's earring, Indigo ran out onto the veranda. She saw that the earring had come to rest in a flowerpot. She quickly scooped it up from the flowerpot, wiped it off, and held it up to the moonlight to inspect it. Fortunately, it appeared unharmed and as sparkly as ever. Relieved, Indigo refastened it to her ear.

She was just turning to re-enter the ballroom when a large and clearly drunken man loomed up alarmingly from the shadows. His name was Lord Lurch and he was no gentleman. Though of a noble family, he had deliberately *not* been invited to the ball, as the king knew him to be a drunken knave and all around scoundrel. Lord Lurch had been lurking in the bushes hoping for exactly such an opportunity to approach the eligible young princess. He was aware of all the dark rumors about her, but they didn't bother him very much. After all, once they were married, he could simply lock her away and claim Abaddon's fortune for himself.

Unfortunately, Indigo now found herself quite alone on the veranda with this awful specimen of manhood. Her inner alarm bell was ringing loudly. She turned quickly, hoping to retreat to safety inside the ballroom. Alas, Lord Lurch cut her off with surprising agility by stepping in front of her.

"Wh…what do you want?" she demanded a bit shakily.

"Don't be frightened, my beauty," he slurred. "I simply want to introduce myself," he bowed low before her, wobbling a bit and took a step closer to her. "Lord Lurch at your service, Princess Indigo," he reached for her silver clad hand, hoping to kiss it.

Repelled, Indigo pulled her hand away before he could grab it. Terrified, she began to back away across the veranda. "Please, don't come any closer!" she pleaded desperately.

Undaunted, the drunken louse continued toward her. "Don't be coy. I'm a great catch," he gloated.

Inside the ballroom, the two Palace Guards who had been assigned to watch the princess were instead gorging themselves at the buffet table. As the first one suddenly thought to make a routine scan of the room, he finally noticed that their charge was missing.

"Where'd our princess go?" he mumbled through a mouth full of cheesy noodles.

"Uh oh," replied the second guard as he popped another raspberry tart into his mouth. "We'd better find her or the king will have our heads." They dashed off in a dither to find the princess.

Outside, Lord Lurch had cornered Indigo at the end of the veranda. "I'm warning you, not another step!" she cried.

Heedless, Lord Lurch grabbed her by the arm.

As Indigo tried to twist out of his grasp, her gauntlet came loose and fell to the ground.

Aghast, Lord Lurch stared at her bared hand with its discolored fingers and blackened fingernails. "What's wrong with your hand?" he gasped in horrified surprise.

She drew her bare hand protectively into her chest, trying to shrink away from him. "Keep back, you mustn't touch me!" she cried.

But Lord Lurch continued to ignore her warning and lunged forward, grabbing her by her bare hand. "You don't scare me…."

He broke off suddenly as he began to shake violently. The skin on his hand had turned a purplish black color, which was quickly spreading over the rest of his body. "What …have…you…done?" he managed to croak haltingly before falling to the ground.

In shock, Indigo watched as an awful black goo began to seep from his mouth and nose.

Unfortunately, the two errant Palace Guards did *not* arrive in the nick of time to prevent Lord Lurch's tragic, if not unwarranted, demise. Instead, they arrived about five seconds too late. Taking in the horrific scene, the first Palace Guard shouted to the other. "Get the king! Go quickly!"

Jolted out of her shocked state, Indigo bent down to retrieve her fallen gauntlet, which she quickly slipped on before turning to flee down the veranda stairs.

A minute later, King Azrael arrived on the veranda along with the second guard. "Oh no!" he cried, staring at the gruesome remains of Lord Lurch. "Where's Princess Indigo?" he demanded, fearing the worst. "Is she all right?"

"I think so," shrugged the second guard. "She ran away when she saw us."

"Quickly, cover the body and dispose of it before anyone sees it. If you value your lives, no one must know about this, understood?" The king looked sharply at the two negligent guards. "If you had watched her as I asked you to, this would never have happened."

The chastened guards hung their heads in shame. "You're right, sir. This is all our fault."

"No, it's not," replied the king morosely. "It's my fault. She was afraid this would happen. And now it has." Devastated, he covered his face with his hands.

Chapter Three

Runaway Princess

Hysterical, Indigo raced through the maze of palace grounds back to sanctuary inside her greenhouse. She dashed inside, bolted the locks, and collapsed with her back against the door. As her legs gave out beneath her, she slid slowly down to the floor.

Nyx immediately trotted over to his distressed mistress, sniffing her worriedly. She pushed him away. "Keep away from me, Nyx! I'm a monster!" she half-shouted, half-sobbed.

Ignoring her command, Nyx nuzzled against her, licking the tears from her cheeks. Indigo threw her arms around the wolf's neck, burying her face in his fur. "We'll stay in here forever, Nyx, just you and me. We don't need anyone else." Nyx nodded his silver head, seeming to agree with her.

* * *

King Azrael knew where he would find his daughter. He took Abigail with him. Knowing he could implicitly trust his longtime maid, he had told her the whole awful truth concerning the demise of the despicable Lord Lurch.

Abigail was distraught for she loved Indigo like her own daughter. Maid and king hurried through the maze-like path down to the greenhouse.

Azrael rapped loudly on the greenhouse door. "Indigo, are you in there?

"Go away, father. I want to be alone," she cried out through the door.

"Are you hurt?" the king asked.

"I'm fine. But Lord Lurch is dead." she stated bluntly. "Are you happy now, Father?"

"It wasn't your fault. I know it was self-defense," the king assured her, feeling dreadfully guilty himself.

"I killed him!" exclaimed Indigo in despair.

The king turned haplessly to Abigail. "Indigo, it's Abigail. I know what happened. Please, let us in so we can talk to you," she pleaded.

"Go away, Abigail. Leave me alone. I'm cursed!" Indigo cried despondently.

"Please, Indigo. Unlock the door and come out," pleaded the king. "We want to help you."

"You can't help me! No one can!" she shouted in despair. "Go away, both of you. Please, just leave me alone."

Abigail sighed and turned to the king. "Let's let her be. There's no reasoning with her when she's like this."

The king also sighed. "I suppose you're right. At least she's safe…for now…"

"She's not going anywhere," confirmed the maid.

Wearily, the king took hold of Abigail's arm and helped her up the long and winding path back to the castle where the ball was still unfortunately in progress. He would have to go back inside the ballroom and extend Indigo's regrets, explaining that she had been overcome by a sudden headache and forced to retire to her chamber. Then he would have to smile at his unsuspecting guests, pretending that all was still well and that the worst had not just happened.

* * *

A dark, eerie looking castle sat high atop a deserted mountain peak. The castle did not look at all prosperous or well tended. The walls were dilapidated and crumbling with mold and age. The surrounding trees were tall, dark, and crooked (much like the castle's occupant). Indeed, the entire area seemed curiously devoid of life, almost as if a fire had passed over it. Nor was there any sign of life inside the dismal castle save for one small light, which flickered from a window high in the derelict central tower.

Inside the castle's lighted window, the aging but still rather dashing sorcerer, Zimbardo, sat in his gloomy laboratory, staring into his black crystal mirror. He wore a long, rather stylish black robe. Around his neck hung a glowing crystal amulet etched with intricate symbols. Gazing into his crystal mirror, Zimbardo was able to very clearly see Indigo sitting on the floor of her greenhouse.

Perched unhappily near Zimbardo was his captive fairy helper, Dash. Like his master, Dash wore a hooded black robe, so that only his face was visible, peeking out from under the hood. It was an appealing, if impish, face set off by glowing grey eyes. The evil sorcerer had tricked the fairy into servitude several years earlier. Zimbardo controlled him via a fairy-sized crystal amulet, which he had placed around his neck and which Dash could not remove without being fatally zapped by the sorcerer.

"Dash, I think it's time that the young princess and I became better acquainted," announced the sorcerer. "I do believe she's even more beautiful than her mother, if that's possible."

Dash nodded reluctantly. Clearly, his loathsome master was about to hatch yet another despicable plot, which he would be expected to execute— or *be* executed!

"Fetch me that book I've been saving for this special occasion. It's in the library."

"Yes, Master," said the fairy. Obediently, Dash flew out of the room into the library, which was a creepy combination of den, dungeon, and storage room. The space was filled with bizarre artifacts, torture devices, and a few eerily incomplete skeletons. A large map of the Five Kingdoms was prominently displayed on one wall. Each kingdom had been circled and pinned by a feathered dart, numbered one through five. The map was

31

frayed around the edges and contained numerous large *X's,* indicating many revisions. Strangest of all, another wall was lined with portraits of Princess Indigo from babyhood to the present.

Hovering beside a tall bookcase, Dash extracted an old, leather-bound volume. Clutching the book, he flew back to the laboratory and handed it to Zimbardo. The sorcerer flipped through the yellowing manuscript until he found the page he wanted. "Perfect, I'll just include a little note," he said. Ripping off a small piece of parchment, he took up a quill and scribbled, "Best regards, Your Secret Admirer."

Pleased with himself, Zimbardo tucked the note into the page as a bookmark. Then he placed the book inside a carved wooden box lying on his table. Selecting a powdered potion from his shelf, the devious sorcerer poured its contents over the box, causing it to glow eerily. Passing his hand over the top, he chanted in an obscure tongue. Black smoke began to materialize until it encircled the box, causing it to rise up into the air.

* * *

Back at Indigo's greenhouse, the forlorn princess sat huddled over her knees with her eyes closed, so she did not immediately notice the black smoke that began to curl into the room.

Growling low in his throat, Nyx ran forward to sniff the smoke but jumped back in alarm at a sudden very loud thump.

Indigo's head whipped up. As the smoke cleared, they saw that a small wooden box had mysteriously appeared in the middle of the greenhouse floor.

Nyx approached the box, sniffing it warily while Indigo leapt to her feet to investigate.

"That's strange. Where did that come from?" she wondered.

Nyx nosed the box, growling suspiciously.

As Indigo moved toward the box, the wolf stepped in front of her, attempting to block her. "Nyx, don't be silly. It's just a box."

While the wolf shook his head urgently, she bent over to pick up the strange wooden box and carried it over to her worktable. Carefully, she opened the box and lifted out the book, which was lying inside. Intrigued, she opened it up to the marked page. "What's this?" she wondered as she

32

pulled out the note tucked inside.   "Best Regards, Your Secret Admirer," she read in surprise. "Who would admire *me?*" she said dubiously.

She set aside the curious note and studied the page that had been marked.   She read the heading at the top of the page. "*A Cure All for Curses.* Hmm…that's interesting…" She scanned the list of ingredients for the *Cure All*. "Looks like I already have everything I need except some Life Everlasting and water from the Sacred Well of Acheron, wherever that is."

She pondered intrigued. "I wonder if this *Cure All for Curses* could work for me, Nyx?"   She looked at the silver wolf, who solemnly shook his head from side to side. "But, Nyx, I have to try everything. Maybe it won't work, but what if this really is a cure and, by some good fortune, it's landed right here almost in my lap? Maybe it's my destiny.   I have to find out!"

Indigo had made up her mind. She would set off immediately in search of the two items she needed for the *Cure All*. Besides, there was no point in staying in Abaddon any longer. If she couldn't find a cure for her curse, she would have to remain alone forever. She could not risk another terrible accident happening.

She felt awful about Lord Lurch even if he had been a wretched man. She couldn't help feeling terribly guilty even though she knew it was not really her fault. She had warned him repeatedly to stay away from her, but he had drunkenly chosen to ignore her warnings. He had threatened her and then forcibly grabbed her. Obviously, his boorish behavior had precipitated his own death.   She knew that she had done all that she could to prevent it, and that she had not intentionally harmed him.   Still…if she didn't have this ghastly curse, he'd still be alive…

Indigo glanced down at herself, realizing she was still wearing the blue ball gown. "Oh dear, this won't do,'" she said aloud.   She crossed to a small closet at the side of the greenhouse and rifled through it, pulling out several items more appropriate for travel, including a long, hooded cape.

She stepped out of the indigo ball gown, leaving it pooled on the greenhouse floor, and slipped on a simple dress of emerald green wool. Though rather plain in design, it featured a gold trim around the neck and hemline and was quite becoming on her.   Then she exchanged her high-heeled slippers for a pair of sturdy boots. Lastly, she tied the velvet cape of midnight blue around her neck. Now she was ready for travel.

She inspected herself in the mirror-like wall of the greenhouse. In her reflection, she noted that she was still wearing her mother's sparkling earrings. She raised a hand, intending to remove the earrings and put them away for safekeeping. Then she thought better of it. She decided she would wear her mother's earrings in hopes that they would bring her good luck on her journey.

Quickly, she grabbed up a large satchel and threw in all the items she would need for her journey, including herbs, crystals, bottled potions, and the few extra clothes she had pulled from the closet. Fortunately, she had a half-eaten loaf of bread and some nuts and apples to take along so she wouldn't starve. Finally, she picked up the mysterious book and placed it carefully inside her travel bag.

She stood hesitantly, glancing around the greenhouse. "I think that's everything…" she said uncertainly, though she had the feeling she was forgetting something. "Oh . . ." she said, suddenly remembering. Crossing to her garden, she plucked a few herbs and tucked them into the heel of her right boot. "There," she said. "Five blades of yarrow, one to the spirits," she cast a blade over her shoulder. "And a sprig of Angelica to keep us safe from evil." Now she was ready to leave.

From high in his mountaintop castle, Zimbardo peered into his black crystal mirror, intently watching Indigo as she prepared for her journey. "Silly girl," he chuckled. "Your little charms are no match for my powers."

Sitting nearby, Dash looked on, shaking his head grimly. He almost felt sorry for the innocent girl…almost…

Clutching her travel bag, Indigo crossed to the door of the greenhouse. "Come on, Nyx, it's time to go."

The silver wolf growled softly and took hold of Indigo's cape with his teeth, attempting to pull her back from the door.

"Nyx, stop it. We have to leave now while everyone's asleep."

But Nyx stood his ground, stubbornly shaking his head at her.

"Fine," she said, exasperated. "You can stay here if you want to, but I'm going." Resolutely, she unbolted the door and stepped outside.

Reluctantly, Nyx trotted out after her.

"Good boy," she said, patting him affectionately. "You know I'd be lost without you." She closed the greenhouse door and they set off together.

* * *

Peering through his crystal mirror, Zimbardo watched with satisfaction as Indigo and Nyx left the greenhouse. "Good girl," he gloated. "I knew you couldn't resist." Suddenly, his crystal mirror started to glitch, causing his screen to flicker with static and then go black. "No, no, no! Don't die on me now!" cried the frustrated sorcerer. He pounded the screen impatiently. "Damn crystal mirror! I hate this new technology. Dash, get the Crystal Guy now!" he ordered furiously.

* * *

Cautiously, Indigo and Nyx made their way through the nighttime forest, which was full of scary snarls and growls. All around them unidentified bright eyes, big and small, peered curiously at them from the trees. It was most unusual to see anyone traveling at this hour of the night. An owl hooted loudly as they passed under its perch in a large oak tree. Indigo jumped and clutched at Nyx beside her.

"Relax, Nyx, it's just an owl," she said, more for her own benefit. "I don't believe all those stories about the forest being full of man-eating creatures and monsters." A sudden bloodcurdling cry interrupted her. "Oh yes, I do!" she cried.

Overcome with fright, she dropped to her knees and wrapped her arms around Nyx, who licked her reassuringly. Now that she was actually in the middle of the scary nighttime forest, she was having some second thoughts. Perhaps she *had* been a bit hasty and should have thought things through a bit more before leaving. On the other hand, there was no point in going back to Abaddon. If there was any chance at all that this *Cure All* would work, she had to take the chance. She would simply have to be very brave— and stay very close to Nyx, who she knew would never willingly leave her side.

Rising to her feet with new resolve, Indigo continued through the forest, keeping a grounding hand on the wolf's back as they walked. Fortunately, there was a full moon that night, so there was at least some light.

Shortly, they came upon a signpost, which gave them four choices: *Bog of Death, Very High Cliff, Dragon Lair, and Zozimo's Potions.* As the first three options were highly undesirable, Indigo and Nyx set off in the direction of *Zozimo's Potions*.

"Come on, Nyx, maybe this Zozimo will have the herb that I need," she said hopefully. They continued down the path to *Zozimo's Potions*.

* * *

Abigail discovered Indigo's absence early the next morning when she went to deliver some breakfast to the princess. King Azrael was beside himself with worry and self-reproach. What a fool he had been to host a ball before Indigo was ready. Worse, he had left her alone in the greenhouse, believing she was safe. Now she was gone.

Morosely, he sat on his throne, gazing up at the portrait of the late queen. "I fear I've made a mess of things, Citrine. But don't worry, I promise I'll find our girl."

The king's guardsmen rushed into the throne room. "Any news?" the king asked hopefully.

They shook their heads. "Sorry, sir. No sign of her anywhere in the kingdom."

"Well, she can't have gone far. Take as many men as you need and don't come back until you've found her," he ordered.

"Yes, sir!" He and the other guardsmen rushed outside. They jumped onto their waiting horses and set off at a rapid pace into the forest. They were accompanied by numerous hunting dogs, which had been given Indigo's scent from one of her garments.

* * *

Back in the forest, Indigo and Nyx continued on their way when the wolf's ears pricked up suddenly, causing him to growl. "What is it, Nyx?" she asked, glancing around fearfully.

A moment later, they both heard a thunderous noise fast approaching them.

"Run!" shouted Indigo.

Leaving the path, they fled into the forest.   They paused momentarily upon coming to a small stream. Nyx nudged her into the water. Fortunately, it proved to be shallow, and they quickly splashed their way across.

Upon reaching the other side, Nyx saw that his mistress was beginning to tire. Bending low, he deftly scooped her onto his back and continued running through the forest.

The terrifying sounds came from the king's guardsmen, horses, and dogs as they crashed their way through the forest in pursuit of the runaway Princess Indigo. The guardsmen pulled up when they reached the stream. However, the small stream now looked more like a raging river. The dogs halted at the side of the churning river and sniffed the air, uncertain now which way to go.

"Drat it all! They've lost her scent," said the Head Guardsmen, who had spoken with the king. "We'll have to spread out," he said. Obediently, the riders set off in all directions in hopes of discovering the princess.

* * *

In his laboratory, Zimbardo peered through his crystal mirror, watching the guardsmen disperse. "They'll never find her now," he chuckled.

Dash lounged nearby, looking disinterested. He'd already seen that trick twice before.

After the guardsmen had departed, Zimbardo nodded at the mirror, causing the roaring river to once more become a small stream. "Now…let's see where our princess has gone," he said, peering into the black crystal mirror. However, before he could locate her, the mirror began to glitch once again and then went dark.

"Blasted crystal! Dash, get that bloody Crystal Guy back here. Tell him I'm going to make soup with his bones if he doesn't fix it this time!"

When Dash failed to respond immediately, Zimbardo rubbed the crystal amulet around his neck, causing Dash's identical, though much smaller, amulet to light up with electrical energy, giving the fairy a nasty little shock.

"Remember, while I hold this amulet, you cannot disobey me," the sorcerer reprimanded him.

Still vibrating from the electric shock, the fairy leapt to his feet. "Yesss, Master!"

"Get him now!" ordered the frustrated Zimbardo. "Before we lose her."

Dash flew out of the room to fetch the Crystal Guy.

Zimbardo glowered in frustration at his malfunctioning mirror. It was getting embarrassing. Despite his great powers, he could not seem to keep the wretched thing in working order. He had tried everything he could think of to restart it, including shaking, tapping, kicking, and zapping it to no avail.

Dash returned a short while later with the reluctant Crystal Guy, whom he had to forcibly push into the room. He was a fat, balding man wearing a tunic embroidered with the logo, *Crystal Repairs*. All kinds of crystals and gadgets dangled from the man's tool belt, which hung around his ample waist.

"Fix it—or else!" ordered Zimbardo.

The Crystal Guy nervously examined the crystal mirror, afraid to disappoint the sorcerer. At length, he timidly replied, "Sorry, sir, but I can find nothing wrong with this mirror."

To demonstrate, he tapped the mirror with a test crystal then held it up to his ear. The crystal hummed loudly throughout the room. "You see the reception is good, so I think someone must be jamming your channel," he suggested to the glowering sorcerer.

"Jamming my channel? How is that possible?" he demanded in disbelief.

The Crystal Guy shrugged. "Must be someone with very strong warding magic."

"That's impossible!" exclaimed the arrogant sorcerer. "No one's powers are stronger than mine."

The hapless Crystal Guy shrugged again. "Sorry, there's nothing more I can do."

"Well, that's a shame because that makes you absolutely worthless. " The sorcerer snapped his fingers at the captive fairy.

"Dash, would you please see this gentleman *out?*" He nodded his head meaningfully towards the open window.

Taking the hint, Dash flew over to the man and sprinkled him with a little fairy dust, which made even the over-sized Crystal Guy light enough to lift. With ease, Dash hoisted the unfortunate repair man over his shoulder and dropped him out of the castle window, which overlooked the steep mountainside.

Dash grimaced as the poor man screamed and rolled all the way down the mountain, which was a very long way.

"Surely, there must be someone in the Five Kingdoms who can fix a simple crystal mirror," exploded the frustrated sorcerer.

"Sorry, Master," said Dash. "There's no one left."

"Incompetent idiots!" cried Zimbardo. "All right, we'll have to do it the old-fashioned way. Dash, I want you to follow the princess, but be sure to stay out of sight and follow my instructions…exactly!"

"Yes, Master…no offense…but with all the princesses in all the Five Kingdoms, why do you want the one that's cursed?"

Angered by the impertinent question, Zimbardo zapped the fairy again with his amulet.

"Oww!" cried Dash as the electric shock coursed once more through his tiny body, causing him to shake uncontrollably.

"Never question me again, you impudent termite," warned the sorcerer.

* * *

Back in the forest, Nyx was still running at top speed with Indigo clinging to his back.

"Slow down, Nyx. I think we've lost them," she said.

The silver wolf scanned the forest for intruders. Seeing no one, he slowed his pace.

"It's okay, Nyx. You can put me down now."

Nodding, he came to a stop and Indigo slid off his back.

She stood, scanning the dark and foreboding forest, which surrounded them on all sides. "Where are we? We've lost the path," she said anxiously.

Nyx murmured and nudged Indigo, pointing his snout at something in the distance. Indigo followed his gaze and finally caught sight of a small light, glimmering through the trees in the middle of the forest. "Good boy, Nyx. Let's go find out who's there," she said already heading off in the direction of the small light. "I just hope they're friendly," she added with some trepidation.

* * *

The light was coming from Zozimo's small potion shop. As the hour was late, the shop was closed to customers. Inside the shop, Zozimo and Ion were busy concocting potions in the backroom. The bat, Bijou, hung nearby from the rafters, catching a bat nap.

Zozimo stirred a large, bubbling cauldron. "All right, I think this healing potion is almost done," said the wizard. "Ion, fetch me a phoenix feather and some ground lizard's feet."

Dutifully, Ion ran to the crowded shelves to grab the requested ingredients. In his haste, he accidentally grabbed the bottle next to the ground lizard's feet, which was unfortunately *ground dragon's tongue.*

As Zozimo stirred the pot, Ion unwittingly poured the dragon's tongue into the brew. Immediately, it started to bubble up alarmingly.

"Whoa!" said Ion. "Is it supposed to do that?"

"No!" shouted the wizard. "Better run for it."

Just as they reached the door, a huge explosion erupted behind them, propelling them both through the door and onto the grass outside the shop. Black smoke billowed out of the shop windows and door and up through the chimney.

Coughing on the smoke, Bijou flapped his way outside and flew to safety in a nearby tree.

Ion helped the aging wizard to his feet. "Are you all right?" the boy queried solicitously. They were both covered, head to foot, in soot and a sticky, multi-colored gunk.

"Yes, yes, I'm all right," the wizard waved him away impatiently. "Nothing a long bath won't fix. What in seven hells did you put in there?" he demanded.

Ion rubbed the soot from his eyes and examined the bottle he still clutched. "Eww," he said sheepishly. "I accidentally grabbed the powdered dragon's tongue…my bad," he added, lamely.

"Dragon's tongue! Dragon's tongue causes things to blow up! I asked for lizard's feet," scolded the wizard.

"Sorry, I mix up my reptiles," confessed Ion.

"Dragon's have more of a kick," the wizard replied.

"Tell me about it!" said a young, feminine voice behind them.

Startled, Zozimo and Ion whirled around to see a lovely young woman in a long blue cape and a large silver wolf staring at them. The sight was so unexpected, that they were both momentarily speechless.

"Is this a bad time?" asked the girl.

"Kind of," said the surprised wizard. "And you would be?"

"Oh, sorry. I'm In…dia. And this is my wolf, Nyx. I'm a traveling healer," she said, thinking it prudent to hide her true identity.

Ion stepped forward eager to make her acquaintance. "Very pleased to meet you, India. My name is Ion and this grumpy old man is Zozimo. That's Bijou up there in the tree," he pointed upward.

The bat waved a wing at the girl, who waved back.

Zozimo eyed the girl, closely "*India*, is it?" he asked.

The girl nodded, "Yes, India . . .you know, like the big country, India?" She spread her gauntleted hands wide. She was not used to lying and blushed a little at her unaccustomed deception.

Zozimo raised a brow, skeptically. "Well…India…you shouldn't be traveling alone. It's very dangerous in the forest."

"Nyx takes care of me," she smiled and patted the wolf on his head.

Nyx nodded proudly at the pair as though confirming his status as her guardian and protector.

Ion bent to pat Nyx as well, but the wolf growled and nipped his fingers. "Ouch!" he said, pulling away his injured fingers. "Not very friendly, is he?"

"Sorry, I told you he's very protective." She turned to admonish the wolf. "These are friends, Nyx. Hopefully, they can help us, so please be nice…and no biting!"

Nyx nodded but still looked warily at the apparently friendly young man.

"Come along, Ion," said the wizard. "Thanks to you, we've got some clean up to do." Zozimo hurried back inside the shop.

Ion turned to the girl. "Please, come in. Just excuse the mess. We had a
Small…uh…accident," he said ruefully.

Politely, he held open the door for her and Indigo stepped into the shop.

Nyx was just about to follow his mistress when Zozimo called out, "No dogs inside. That goes for wolves."

Indigo turned to her devoted wolf companion, "Don't worry, Nyx. You stay out here. I'll be fine."

Grumbling, Nyx curled up on the front porch as they went inside.

The interior of the shop was an awful mess. The walls were blackened with soot and dripping with the same sticky, multi-colored gunk that clung to Ion's clothes and face. Indigo examined the colorful gunk with some amazement. "Wow! Did you kill a rainbow in here or something?" she asked in disbelief.

"Rainbow? Don't be ridiculous," said the wizard scornfully. Discreetly, he hid a jar labeled with a rainbow and placed it back on a shelf.

Indigo pitched in gamely to help the pair clean up their shop, which fortunately didn't take long inasmuch as Zozimo was able to use a cleaning potion to make most of the gunk magically disappear.

Finally, the shop was spic and span once more. Ion knelt down on the hearth of the rustic stone fireplace to restart the fire, as it had been blown out by the explosion. Indigo moved close to the now glowing hearth, grateful for its warmth.

Zozimo gazed about his shop with satisfaction. "That's better. Let's try to keep things tidy, shall we, Ion?"

Ion glanced up at him from the hearth, grimacing with embarrassment. "No more dragon's tongue, I promise."

"Good," he said pointedly.

Indigo was now wandering about the shop, checking the floor to ceiling shelves, which were enviously full of every possible medicinal herb and potion, many of which she was not familiar.

Zozimo turned his attention to the curious girl, who seemed to be searching for something. "Can I help you with anything?" he inquired.

"I hope so," said Indigo. "Do you have any Life Everlasting in stock?"

"Life Everlasting...a popular request...I may be out," he frowned uncertainly.

"Oh, I hope not!" she exclaimed. "I really, really need it!"

Zozimo scanned his shop ledger, which itemized his entire stock. "Hold on. You may be in luck," he said. He moved off to check his shelves and returned moments later, holding aloft a small vial of the rare herb. "You got the last one," he said. "It must have been waiting for you. Things like this happen for a reason you know," said the canny wizard.

"Oh, thank you!" exclaimed Indigo with obvious relief. "I don't know what I'd do if you didn't have it. Now I just need some water from the Sacred Well of Acheron. I don't suppose you have that too?" she asked hopefully.

The wizard's attitude changed. He eyed her sharply. "What do you want with that?" he asked, looking quite grim.

Indigo shrugged vaguely. "I need it for a...healing potion I'm working on."

"I don't have it in stock," said the wizard, "And, I warn you, it's not easy to come by. The Sacred Well of Acheron is located in the Valley of Vervain. It's at least a three day's journey on foot."

"Perhaps I could ride?" she suggested. "I'm a good horsewoman."

The wizard shook his head. "That's not advisable, I fear. Horses get very skittish in the Haunted Forest."

"Haunted Forest?" she asked worriedly.

The wizard nodded affirmatively. "And, of course, the well is guarded by The Serpent of Minerva. It's very choosy about who gets water from the well."

"Serpent?" repeated Indigo, now looking even more worried. "Is that like a large snake?"

The wizard nodded and stretched his arms very wide. "He's a monster and he doesn't like visitors. He's been known to swallow them whole ...if he's displeased with their request," he added ominously.

"Oh dear," said Indigo, now looking very worried indeed. "It would defeat the whole purpose if I were to be eaten. But without water from the Sacred Well, I can't very well make my cure ...er...potion. So I must at least try."

The wizard eyed her knowingly. "Yes, I understand your dilemma. But it's too dangerous to let you travel alone. Ordinarily, I'd be happy to go with you, but I can't leave the shop just now. It's plague season, you know."

Indigo sighed heavily. "Now what?" she wondered aloud.

"I have a way with reptiles," said Ion, not altogether truthfully. "I'd be happy to go with you," he volunteered, turning to Zozimo. "If you can spare me that is…"

"Not really," the wizard shook his head. "But she can't go alone. Take Bijou with you. He knows the way."

Perched high in the shop rafters, the bat looked surprised and not altogether pleased to hear himself nominated for the dangerous mission. Nonetheless, he was highly responsible and conscientious and enjoyed being of service to his wingless friends, so he shrugged gamely and nodded his assent.

"Bijou is an excellent guide. You can trust him," he told Indigo. "You can stay the night and leave in the morning."

"Oh thank you," said Indigo fervently. "It's very kind of all of you to offer to help me. Unfortunately, I have no money to pay you for your service."

"No payment is required," the wizard assured her. "It's good karma to help those in need."

Ion nodded. "Personally, I'll be happy to get out of this stuffy shop. Anyway, I'd rather face a serpent than catch the plague."

"Humph," said the wizard. "I can treat the plague, but I can't extract you from the belly of a serpent."

"Oh well," shrugged Ion manfully. "I'll take my chances. Besides, someone has to go with India. Bijou can't help her if she gets into trouble."

"That's very brave and gallant of you," said Indigo. She thought she would feel very safe with this tall and charming young man at her side.

"I'm at your service," Ion declared, blushing a bit. He hoped she couldn't read his true thoughts, as he wasn't volunteering just to be gallant. It was more of an excuse to spend more time with this intriguing and daring young woman who had such amazing blue eyes. No, he was not going to mind this journey one little bit…

"Bijou," Zozimo addressed the bat. "Would you please take India up to the guest attic—and make sure it's rodent free."

He handed Indigo a small vial of murky green liquid. "Use this potion, if need be," he instructed her.

Bijou started to lead the way upstairs, but Indigo stood frozen in her tracks, staring at the sickening green liquid floating inside the vial. "I'm not very fond of rodents," she said worriedly.

"Either am I," said the wizard. Lately, we've had a terrible infestation of fanged blue rats. I suspect they may be carriers of the plague, though I can't prove it."

"Oh dear," said Indigo. "Maybe I can just sleep here by the fire—or outside with Nyx."

"Nonsense!" said the wizard. "The rat potion is very effective. Why, I haven't seen one of the little *fangers* in two or three days now. If you see any little eyes staring at you in the dark, just splash some of the potion on them and it should melt them straightaway."

Indigo looked aghast as she stared at the bilious green potion. "Does it *melt* people too?" she asked.

Zozimo raised his brows. "Well, I haven't tried that yet…just to be safe, try not to spill any on yourself. "

Indigo still looked uncertain and hesitated to follow Bijou up the narrow staircase that led to the attic.

"If you like, I'll be happy to go up with you and make sure it's safe," offered Ion.

"Oh, yes, I'd appreciate that very much," Indigo gushed with relief.

Smiling reassuringly, Ion lit a candle at the fireplace and started up the slightly rickety staircase.

Gratefully, Indigo followed him and Bijou up the stairs.

"Hurry back, Ion," the wizard called after them. "There are a few things I need to go over with you before you undertake the journey."

Indigo turned back to Zozimo. "Perhaps I should stay as well?" she asked.

The wizard waved his hand dismissively, shooing her upstairs. "No, no, nothing you need to worry about …just a few *technicalities* I need to review with Ion—privately."

"Oh…" she turned back and continued to follow Ion up the staircase.

Up in the attic, Ion set the candle into a holder, illuminating the small room. Evidently, Zozimo used it for storage, as well as guests, as there were numerous bulging bags stacked about the room and some of them smelled a bit unpleasant. She guessed that the sacks contained the ingredients for the wizard's many potions. In a small alcove there stood a rustic dresser and bed, which was made up with a cozy looking quilt.

Indigo gazed about the small attic in trepidation, expecting to be attacked momentarily by a fanged blue rat. "Do you see any rats?"

Bijou zipped about the room, checking all of the corners, both high and low. While he found no rats of any color, he did encounter a number of tasty insects, which he quickly devoured for his bedtime snack.

Holding the candlestick, Ion got down on his hands and knees and also peered into the dark corners. Satisfied he got to his feet. "All clear," he pronounced. He turned to the bat. "What do you think, Bijou?"

As he and Indigo looked on, Bijou popped a nasty-looking spider into his mouth and smacked his lips approvingly.

Ion made a face. "Sorry I asked."

He turned back to the girl. "Don't worry, I normally sleep up here, and I have yet to see one fanged blue rat."

"Well, that's good to know," said Indigo, feeling a bit better about her sleeping quarters. "But if I'm taking your bed, where are you going to sleep?"

Ion shrugged. "Don't worry, I'm perfectly happy to roll up by the fire."

Indigo held up the green potion in the palm of her gauntlet. "Do you think I'll have to use this?"

Ion laughed. "I never did. Don't worry, it's just a precaution. Zozimo can be a bit over dramatic."

"I feel terrible about taking your bed," she told him. "I'd offer to share but..."

Ion blushed in the dark. "That's very kind of you, but I don't think Zozimo would approve."

"That's *not* what I meant!" She blushed even redder than Ion, hoping she hadn't given him the wrong idea about her!

Ion's mouth twisted, as though he were trying not to laugh. "No, worries! Well, better get some sleep. We have a big day tomorrow."

Turning quickly, he galloped back downstairs, taking two at a time. He thought she was adorably awkward and nice and did not want to hurt her feelings by laughing in her face.

With a wave of his wing, Bijou flew off hurriedly after Ion.

Was it her imagination, or was even the bat laughing at her?

Oh great! she groaned to herself.   Ion was the first really attractive guy she had ever met, and now he probably thought she was a gibbering idiot—or worse!

From below, Ion's laughter floated up the stairs.

Humiliated, Indigo fell over onto the bed and pulled the pillow over her head.

Chapter Four

The Haunted Forest

The next morning dawned a bit chilly and overcast. A fog had settled over the surrounding forest but was already beginning to lift as the sun crept over the horizon. Indigo and Ion stepped out of Zozimo's shop, looking rested and ready for travel. Indigo wore her green gown under the dark blue cape and clutched her satchel full of precious potions and herbs. Ion had borrowed a warm woolen cloak from Zozimo for the trip and looked a great deal more dashing in it than the wizard ever had.

Still curled up on the front porch, Nyx leapt to his feet to greet his mistress, licking her affectionately on the face. "I missed you, too," she laughed as the wolf bathed her face in kisses. "I told you I'd be okay."

Keeping a judicious distance, Ion waved a greeting to the large wolf. "Hey there, Big Guy," he said respectfully. Unimpressed, Nyx grunted softly in reply to let the boy know he was still keeping an eye on him.

Zozimo emerged from the shop with Bijou on his shoulder. He handed a bulging sack to Ion. "I packed some provisions, as well as a few potions and herbs, just in case you meet with the...uh...*unexpected*..."

"Thanks," said Ion, patting the knapsack already on his back. "I brought a few things as well . . .just in case we meet…well, you know…" He glanced at Indigo and let his voice trail off.

Indigo looked warily between the wizard and his apprentice. "Is there something you're not telling me?" she asked.

"No, no," Ion shook his head, "Nothing for you to worry about. It's just better to be prepared in case of…emergencies."

"You're expecting *emergencies*?" she asked the tall boy. "Like what?"

"Well, frankly, you never know who…or what…we might encounter on our path. There's—"

Zozimo intervened, cutting off Ion before he could name any specific worrisome creatures. "Don't worry, my lady. You're in good hands with Ion and Bijou—so to speak," he said, glancing at the bat's wings. "Just make sure you stick to the path and stay together," the wizard cautioned her.

"Yes, sir, I will. Thank you again for all of your help and for allowing Ion and Bijou to accompany me. I hope to pay you back one day," she said gratefully.

"Just come back safely….all of you," he told the traveling party. He raised a hand and chanted a protective blessing upon the young travelers.

Ion turned to Indigo. "Ready?" he asked her.

Indigo nodded while patting Nyx. "We're ready," she said.

"Good, we should leave before the dragons wake up."

Indigo's eyes flew wide. So did Nyx's. "*Dragons*?" she asked, alarmed.

Zozimo scowled at his overly frank assistant. "Go along now. Bijou, lead the way and be my eyes. Report back to me…if need be…"

Nodding at his master, Bijou leapt off the wizard's shoulder and flew off ahead of the travelers into the forest.

"Hey, wait for us," shouted Ion as he, Indigo, and Nyx hurried off in the direction of the speedy bat.

"Oh, Ion, one more thing…" Zozimo waved back his young assistant.

Leaving Indigo's side, Ion ran back to Zozimo. "Yes, sir?" he asked, eager to be on his way.

The wizard lowered his voice, "Keep a close eye on the girl and protect her from harm," he said sternly. "But whatever you do, don't touch her bare hands!"

Ion nodded, looking quizzically at the wizard. "Why?" he asked.

"Just do as I say. Go now, they're waiting for you." He waved off Ion, who gave the wizard another questioning look before running back to rejoin the traveling party.

Bijou led the travelers over a rather treacherous, overgrown path through the woods. They encountered nothing out of the ordinary until they came upon a signpost that announced, *YOU ARE NOW ENTERING THE HAUNTED FOREST.* Peering anxiously beyond the signpost into The Haunted Forest, Indigo thought it looked very dark and dense inside and… well… *haunted!* She could hear numerous snarls and growls, emanating from inside the fearful woods.

"Do we really have to go through the Haunted Forest?" Indigo asked, turning to Bijou, who was perched atop the signpost. The bat nodded. "There's no other way?" she pressed. Glumly, the large bat shook his head and then flew off ahead of them into the Haunted Forest.

"Looks like we don't have any choice," shrugged Ion. "Don't worry, it's not so bad. I've been inside a few times on errands for Zozimo. You just have to keep your eyes open…"

"Did you see anything like…say…man-eating monsters?" she asked worriedly.

"Don't worry," Ion assured her. "They're mostly a lot of *boo* and no bite."

Cautiously, the trio entered the Haunted Forest. As soon as they stepped inside, the dark woods seemed to close in around them. Indigo could see numerous bright eyes, large and small, staring back at her. A creature, which looked like a toothy, overgrown raccoon, jumped out in front of her, causing her to shriek in alarm. Growling fiercely, Nyx lunged at the creature, who melted back quickly into the forest.

Badly frightened, Indigo crouched down, wrapping her arms around the silver wolf. "Good boy, Nyx," she praised him. She turned to Ion, "What in the world was that?"

"Looked like a mutated raccoon," he told her. "But don't worry, most of them are harmless."

"Most of them?" echoed Indigo. "What about the ones who aren't?"

"Don't worry, I'll take care of them," Ion promised boldly.

Nyx barked as if to remind the boy that it was he who had scared off the creature.

Smiling weakly, Indigo rose to her feet. "Sorry, I'm a little jumpy," she said apologetically. "I don't get out much."

"I thought you were a traveling healer," he said.

"Well…I am but I usually stay out of the woods," she replied, trying not to blow her cover.

They resumed walking side by side through the dense forest. Nyx followed closely behind them, keeping a vigilant eye on the surrounding trees.

"Will it really take us three days to get to the Valley of Vervain?" Indigo asked.

"Hopefully not," said Ion. "Zozimo's so slow it takes him a full three days. We can move a lot faster, so we should be able to do it in two… unless we run into dragons. Or God forbid, goats…"

"*Goats?* You're afraid of goats?" she asked in surprise.

"Trust me," Ion said, a bit defensively. "These are no ordinary goats. They have blood red eyes, huge sharp horns, and—" Something rustled in the woods behind them.

Warily, Indigo turned to look behind them. "Sharp teeth?" she asked nervously.

"Good guess," he said.

Abruptly, Bijou zoomed up in front of Ion, urgently pointing a wing at something behind him.

Indigo was also mutely pointing a finger behind her. Belatedly, Ion turned around just as a dozen mutated goats with blood red eyes, long, sharp horns, and razor sharp teeth jumped from the bushes and surrounded them from the rear.

"Is that them?" Indigo asked in a weak voice.

"That's them!" confirmed Ion. "Run for it!"

Bijou zoomed off ahead of them, searching for an escape route, while Ion and Indigo ran for their lives after the bat. Growling, Nyx stood his ground, bravely attempting to confront the toothsome goats, but quickly realized that even a large wolf was no match for a pack of crazed goats with bloodlust in their crimson eyes. Turning tail, Nyx fled off down the path after his mistress. Upon reaching her, he bent low, scooped her up onto his back, and tore off down the trail after Bijou.

The goats were now almost upon Ion and gave him a few fanny pokes with their large, sharp horns. "Ouch!" he cried, finding the adrenaline to run quite a bit faster down the path.

Ion burst out of the woods with the slavering goats still in hot pursuit. Ahead of him, he saw that the other travelers were stopped at the side of a roaring river full of dangerously churning rapids.

"Hurry!" called Indigo, fearing that Ion was about to become *lunchmeat* for the closely pursuing and obviously hungry goats.

Finally, Ion outpaced the encroaching goat posse and reached Bijou and Indigo, waiting at the side of the churning river. "What now?" he panted.

Bijou lifted a wing, pointing to a rickety wooden bridge with rope sides, which swayed perilously over the threatening river.

"We'll have to cross. It's our only chance!" Ion shouted over the roar of the river.

As they considered their options, rotted planks began to fall off the ancient bridge into the churning rapids below.

"It doesn't look safe," cried Indigo anxiously.

"Do they?" Ion nodded his head at the still pursuing goats, who were now almost upon them at the side of the river.

Without further deliberation, Bijou led the travelers onto the swaying bridge. They ran as fast as they could over the crumbling structure, clinging onto the rope sides for dear life. Even so, it was very difficult to keep their footing on the constantly zigzagging bridge. One false step and they would be plunged into the frothing, rock-filled water below doubtless to be swept to their doom over a fearsome waterfall, which they could hear roaring in the distance.

Ion brought up the rear, running behind Indigo to make sure she didn't slip on the buckling bridge. Glancing over his shoulder, he was dismayed to see that the relentless creatures were closing fast. Fortunately, some of the goats had already lost their footing on the slippery bridge and had fallen into the churning water. However, the remaining goats were now almost upon them.

Before they could reach him, Ion turned with a shout and managed to knock several from the bridge. Undeterred, the next goat leapt upon him, almost knocking him over. Ion managed to wrestle off the crazed creature and flung it over the side of the bridge. However, in doing so, he lost his footing and tumbled over the side as well.

Hearing his shout, Indigo turned around and gasped in horror. Ion was barely clinging to the bottom of the rope bridge.

"Hang on, Ion, I'm coming," she cried. Kneeling down, she grabbed hold of his hand with her silver gauntlets; however, she was not quite strong enough to pull him up and her gauntlets were beginning to slip...

Seeing his mistress's peril, Nyx dashed to the rescue, grabbing hold of Ion's arm with his teeth and hauling him back onto the bridge. With no time to lose, Indigo jumped onto Nyx's back, while Ion grabbed hold of the wolf's tail. Nyx shot across the swaying rope structure with Ion dragging along behind them.

They made it the rest of the way across the bridge only moments ahead of the surviving goat pack. Immediately upon reaching the riverbank, Ion pulled an impressive looking dagger from his boot and began sawing frantically through the ropes suspending the bridge. In the nick of time, the severed ropes gave way, sending the remainder of the goat pack to their doom in the raging water.

Utterly exhausted, Indigo and Ion collapsed beside each other on the riverbank. Nyx rested, panting beside them, while Bijou hung upside down in a nearby tree with his wings wrapped over his eyes.

When he had finally caught his breath, Ion rolled toward Indigo, propping himself up on one elbow. "Goats!" he exclaimed in disgust. "I hate goats!"

She nodded in agreement. "I can't imagine anything worse than those horrible creatures!"

"If we're lucky—" said Ion.

She propped herself on an elbow to confront him. "What do you mean *if we're lucky?*" she queried him. "Is there something worse than those crazy goats?"

"Probably not," he shrugged. "But it *is* The Haunted Forest. "

"I hope I live to regret this," she sighed. "It seems I'm endangering your life as well as mine."

"Don't worry about me," said Ion. "I'm always up for a risky adventure. Actually, it's been pretty fun so far. But, I'll take you back if you're afraid…" he looked at her, questioningly.

"No…there's no going back," she said, determinedly. Anyway, except for those goats, I guess it has been kind of *fun*," she smiled at him. For a girl who had spent almost all of her life indoors, this had been quite an adventure.

When they had recovered from their unfortunate goat episode and eaten some lunch, the travelers continued on through the Haunted Forest. On the other side of the river, the forest became almost tropical in appearance. The foliage was lush and green and was full of colorful vining flowers.

"Wow! It's really green in here," marveled Indigo.

"That's because they get a lot of rain," said Ion. "Zozimo warned me to watch out for flash floods."

*"*Flash floods?*"* repeated Indigo worriedly.

Ion scanned the clear blue sky overhead. "Fortunately, I don't see any rain clouds today." He had no sooner spoken than large dark clouds began to drift rapidly into view. "Then again, I may have spoken too soon."

At that moment, the clouds burst open above them, pouring down a sudden, torrential rain. "I've never seen rain like this," said Indigo. "Do you think it might be a flash flood?" As she spoke, the water began to rise above her ankles and rapidly reached her calves.

"I'm guessing that would be a *yes,*" said Ion. "We need to find shelter fast."

The water was now approaching Indigo's waist. Nyx was already treading water. "Help!" cried Indigo as she was suddenly swept off her feet and carried off by the rising water, which now resembled a roaring river.

Howling in distress, Nyx swam after his floating mistress.

Ion was quicker. He dove into the water and with a few long strokes managed to close the distance and grab hold of Indigo. As he was much taller than her, his feet were still able to touch the ground. Wading through the surging water, he carried her to safety up the adjacent hillside.

Bijou zoomed up in front of him. "Did you find shelter?" asked a shivering Ion. The bat nodded urgently, indicating that he should follow him up the hill. The rain continued to lash down upon them as Ion staggered up the steep, water-drenched slope with Indigo in his arms. Nyx loped behind them also having a hard time keeping his footing on the rain-slicked hillside.

Indigo squirmed in Ion's arms. "You can put me down, you know," she said indignantly. "I can walk now."

But he held her fast. "It's way too slippery to risk." As a pretense, he pretended to slip but quickly righted himself. "It's better if I carry you... unless you want to be swept away again?" he looked down questioningly into her pale, wet face.

Mutely, she shook her head. He noted that her intense blue eyes looked even bluer against the cold pallor of her skin. Actually, he probably could put her down safely, but it wasn't everyday he got to carry a beautiful girl in his arms.

Indigo peered up into Ion's face above her. Now that she was so close to him, she could see that his eyes were almost emerald in color and were framed by large dark eyelashes. Momentarily, she forgot that she was in jeopardy and marveled that she was being carried in the strong arms of a very good-looking young man. As she had absolutely no experience with men, other than her father, it was quite a novel and not unpleasant experience. "Where are we going?" she asked anxiously.

"Up the hill," said Ion. "Otherwise, I have absolutely no idea. Hopefully, Bijou knows where he's going."

Flying above him, the bat nodded at Ion and urged him further up the steep slope.

Finally, they arrived at a large opening in the hillside where Ion gently returned Indigo to her feet.

Bijou motioned them inside the opening where they discovered a spacious cave that was tall enough even for Ion to stand up straight.

"Good job, Bijou," Ion praised their resourceful guide. "I'll see if I can get a fire going." He turned to Indigo, "We'd better get out of these wet clothes before we freeze to death."

"C-c-can I help?" she asked with chattering teeth.

He nodded, "Gather up anything that might burn: dry twigs, brush, dead wood ..."

They soon had a large pile of dry tinder, which they scooped together in the center of the cave. Ion extracted a flint from his bag and then pulled the dagger from his boot. By striking his knife on the edge of the flint, he managed to spark a small flame. Carefully, he blew on the embers until they fully ignited. "There," he said, "It'll be toasty in here in no time."

Indigo moved as close to the fire as she dared. "Thank you," she said gratefully. "That feels wonderful."

Nyx shook himself, causing the flying water drops to almost extinguish the fire.

"Easy there," Ion cautioned the wolf.

Grunting apologetically, Nyx eased himself in front of the fire and nuzzled close to Indigo.

As he was not at all the shy type, Ion jumped to his feet by the fire and immediately began stripping off his soaked cloak and shirt.

"What are you doing?" gasped Indigo, shocked to suddenly find a half-naked man standing in front of her. He was more muscular than she had thought. Modestly, she turned her eyes away.

Nyx gave the boy a warning bark.

Realizing his lack of decorum, Ion stopped short of removing his wet pants. "Sorry," he apologized. "I'm not used to the company of women. Back home it's just my parents, my six brothers, and me. My mom says we're hopelessly uncouth. I hope I didn't offend you."

She turned back to face him. "Of course not. Obviously, you can't stay in those wet clothes. I'll turn around while you finish changing. Then you can turn around while I change," she suggested, trying not to stare at his smooth chest with its patch of blonde hair.

"Forgive my manners," he said. "You should change first," he offered.

"No, please, you're already half . . .uh. . .naked," she said trying not to stare at his bare chest.

"I'll be fast," he promised, already starting to lower his wet pants.

Abruptly, Indigo turned her back to him once more. "Let me know when you're done," she said, trying to act like it was no big deal to have a man stripping naked behind her.

Quickly, Ion slipped on some dry clothes from his knapsack. "Okay," he said. "It's your turn."

She turned around to find that he was now wearing a billowy white shirt and a pair of tight leather pants. She thought he looked quite dashing.

"Turn around," she reminded him as he stood grinning down at her.

"Oh, sorry," he said, turning his back to her.

"I trust you are a gentleman and will not peek."

Nyx cocked an eye at him, letting him know he'd better not.

Truth is, if Nyx hadn't been keeping an eye on him, Ion would definitely have been tempted to take a few peeks. Judging by the luscious curves outlined by Indigo's wet dress, he imagined that she probably had a perfect body. Good thing he had a good imagination... While Ion's back was turned to her, Indigo opened her travel bag and pulled out a warm lavender colored gown, which she knew was becoming on her. Quickly, she stepped out of her wet clothes and into the dry gown. "Okay," she announced. "I'm decent."

Ion whirled around and couldn't help staring, as the lavender dress made her eyes look almost purple. "Wow, you look really...nice."

"Thank you," she said. Self-consciously, she crouched down by the fire. "I think I've finally stopped shivering."

He crouched next to her beside the fire, rubbing his hands over the flames.

"Do you think some creature lives here?" Indigo asked, gazing around at the spacious cave interior.

"I hope not..." Ion said a bit tentatively. "I already checked and I didn't see any signs of occupancy."

"Good," said Indigo relieved. "I've had enough rude surprises for one day. "

Nyx grunted and nuzzled his way between his mistress and the tall boy, deliberately interrupting them before they could get too close.

Above them, Bijou had made himself at home and was fast asleep as he hung upside down in the cave rafters.

Crouched beside each other at the fire, Indigo and Ion exchanged glances and awkward smiles. A long silence ensued between the two, who now found themselves cozily ensconced together in the warm cave.

Ion cleared his throat, several times, searching for conversation. He was eager to learn all he could about this most unusual girl.

"So...India, where are you from?" he queried her.

"The Kingdom of Abaddon," she replied.

"Abaddon?" he asked in surprise. "Didn't they just have a big ball there?"

Indigo nodded. "Yes, they did. I was there."

"You were?" asked Ion, wishing now that he hadn't jumped out of that window.

"I'm afraid so," she replied.

"You don't sound very happy about it," he said.

"Let's just say, things could have gone better..." she said vaguely.

"My brothers were there. Maybe you met them?" he asked.

"Maybe," said Indigo. "What are their names?"

"Well, there's six of them: Princes Boron, Neon, Zenon, Argon, Radon, and

Barium...of Beringer," he told her.

"Oh, yes," she recalled. "I think I do remember them. They're...uh... very nice," she said politely.

"Not my brothers," he said, chuckling. "You must be thinking of someone else's brothers."

She laughed with him. "Well, I think I do like *you* the best," she confessed.

"Thanks, although that's not really much of a compliment, knowing my brothers," he said with a smirk.

"Wait a minute," said Indigo, suddenly realizing. " If you're their brother, then you must be..."

Ion leapt to his feet and bowed gallantly before her. "Prince Ion of Beringer at your service, madam."

"You're a prince?" she asked in astonishment. "No offense, but you don't seem very princely."

Ion shrugged. "Sorry, I left my jewels and royal robes back at the castle, although I do have this..." He reached into his boot and pulled out the large dagger that he had earlier used to start the fire and saw through the rope bridge. Carefully, he held it out to her. "Watch you don't cut yourself. It's very sharp."

She clutched the hilt of the dagger with both hands and waved it around a bit, prompting Ion to jump backwards in alarm. "Easy!" he cautioned.

She studied the dagger between her gauntlets and realized it was indeed no ordinary weapon. The hilt was studded with large gems and bore the royal crest of Beringer. Gingerly, she turned it over, marveling at its beauty.

Judiciously, Ion removed the dagger from her hands and tucked it back into his boot.

"So you really are a prince?" she asked with some amazement.

Ion nodded. "I'm afraid so, for all the good it does me. As the youngest of seven brothers, I stand to inherit nothing. That's why I'm apprenticed to Zozimo. I need to learn a trade."

"I see," said Indigo. "So why weren't you at the ball with your brothers?" she inquired curiously.

"Are you kidding? I don't want to marry *Princess Death*!"

Shocked, she gasped and leapt suddenly to her feet, glaring at Ion.

"Hey, what'd I say?" he asked in genuine confusion. He rose to his feet to face her.

"Is *that* what they call me?" she demanded angrily.

"What are you talking about?" He had no idea why she was so upset. "Are you friends with her...or something?" he asked perplexed.

"Or something," she said archly.

Ion watched in amazement as she removed one of her gauntlets, revealing her discolored hand and blackened fingernails. "What's wrong with your hand?" he gasped.

"Follow me...if you dare!" Indigo taunted him. Turning away from him, she strode angrily to the mouth of the cave.

Thoroughly bemused, Ion followed her outside. It had finally stopped raining but was still misty and overcast.

Indigo crossed to a small, scraggly bush that grew near the entrance of the cave. Bending down, she touched the bush with her bare hand, causing it to instantly shrivel up and disintegrate.

"How'd you do that?" Ion asked in disbelief. He really hoped she wasn't a witch.

"It's easy, I'm cursed!" she exclaimed with self-loathing.

"I don't get it," he said, now really confused.

"What don't you get? I'm the evil monster, *Princess Death*!"

He could only gape at her in stunned amazement

59

"You can leave now if you want to. I wouldn't blame you," she said, hanging her head in shame.

For a long moment, he just stared at her. She could see he was shocked but not frightened. "Do you mean me any harm?" Ion asked, looking at her intently.

She lifted her head to return his steady gaze. "Of course not! I would never harm you. I don't want to hurt anyone…or anything. That's why I'm on this quest."

"And you swear you're not a witch?" he had to ask.

"No! I swear to you I'm not a witch. I 'm just cursed," she lamented. "Though I'm not sure which is worse," she hung her head again.

"Well, I wouldn't help you if you were a witch," he said. "But since it's not your fault that you've been cursed, I will stay and help you undo the wrong that has been done to you."

She looked up at him warily. "You will?" she asked.

He nodded his head solemnly. "You can trust me. I'm a man of my word. And I want to help you, India, because I believe you are good and true. " He was afraid he might scare her if he said too much more.

"Thank you for believing in me, Ion. I am fortunate to have your help. But would you please call me Indigo?

"*Indigo* . . .that's a pretty name. . .and the color of your eyes," he noted, staring into them.

"Thank you. My mother named me," she told him.

"So *you're* Princess Death—I mean Princess Indigo!" he marveled. "You're certainly not what I expected," he admitted.

"Why? What did you expect?" she asked, sarcastically. "An ugly witch with the Evil Eye?"

He shrugged. "Kind of…you must know there are a lot of rumors about you. People love to gossip, you know."

"Oh, I know, believe me!" she said with chagrin. "That's why my father decided to hold the ball. He wanted to show everyone that I'm not really a monster." She sighed, heavily. "Boy, was he wrong!" Overcome by emotion, she dropped to the ground and covered her face with her hands.

Concerned, Ion sat beside her. Gingerly, he placed a consoling hand on her back. "Did something happen?"

She nodded grimly. "Something terrible...I killed a man," she confessed. "But I didn't mean to...it was an accident."

"Is that why you ran away?" he asked.

She nodded. "I have to find a cure for this." With disdain, she waved her discolored hand at him. "Or I'll never be able to lead a normal life."

Ion suddenly remembered Zozimo's parting words to him, *Whatever you do, don't touch her bare hands.* "Now I get it!" he said to himself.

"What?" she asked as she pulled her gauntlet back on.

"Nothing," he replied. "Now that the rain has stopped, we should continue on while we still have daylight." He jumped to his feet and unthinkingly offered her his hand. Awkwardly, he withdrew it.

Indigo held up her gauntleted hands. "Don't worry. You can touch me as long as I have these on."

"Oh . . ." he said, embarrassed. Tentatively, he offered her his hand once again. She clasped it with her gauntlet and he pulled her to her feet.

"See? I didn't kill you . . .yet," she said ruefully.

"Works for me," he replied cheerfully.

Chapter Five

Beware the Winged Creatures

Several hours had passed since the travelers had left the cave. They had passed through the dark and gloom of the Haunted Forest without encountering any further threats. At length, they left the forest behind and emerged into the bright sunlight of midafternoon. They were surprised to find themselves staring up at a very high mountain peak that was ringed around the top with snow.

Bijou hovered uncertainly in front of them, seeming to have lost his way.

"Now what?" Ion asked the confused bat. "Zozimo didn't say anything about mountain climbing."

The bat appeared to regain his bearings and zipped off around the side of the mountain.

Shrugging at each other, Ion and Indigo hurried off after the bat while Nyx loped behind them, playfully chasing after a swarm of colorful butterflies that arose from the surrounding tall grass.

Fortunately, they had not gone very far when they found Bijou hovering over a narrow passageway that appeared to cut completely through the mountain.   The sides of the pass were steeply angled and rose up sharply around them.   Motioning for them to follow, the bat flew off through the passageway ahead of them.

"Looks like Bijou found a shortcut," said Ion as he started off after the bat. "Beats walking around the entire mountain."

Indigo nodded with relief. "Finally, something easy." She ruffled Nyx's fur with her gauntlet.   "Come on, Boy."   But the wolf didn't move. Instead, he lifted his snout, sniffing the air suspiciously and gave a low growl. "What is it, Nyx?" The wolf shook his head at her and ran back out of the passageway, indicating that she should follow him.

Ion ran back to see what the problem was. "What's with him?" he asked her.

"I don't know," Indigo said with consternation. "For some reason, he doesn't want to go through the pass."

Bijou had also flown back to see what was holding them up. Ion turned to the bat. "The wolf senses something amiss. Are you sure the pass is safe?" he asked.   Bijou flitted off to do a brief reconnaissance of the area.

 He returned a short while later and nodded at Ion, giving him a rather awkward thumbs up with his webbed wing.

"Bijou says it's safe." He shrugged at Indigo. "Either we go through or we walk around the entire mountain."

"Let's go," she told him resolutely. "I don't want to lose any more time." She motioned to Nyx to rejoin them and then set off after Ion.

Grumbling unhappily, Nyx returned to his mistress's side and reluctantly trotted after her through the narrow mountain pass.

* * *

Zimbardo stood in his sinister laboratory, speaking into the crystal amulet around his neck, which he never removed. Unfortunately, his black crystal mirror, which he had earlier used to spy upon Indigo, was still malfunctioning and, therefore, unusable.   That's why he had to resort to using the relatively low-tech crystal amulet to communicate with his fairy henchman.

"Dash, have you located the princess?" he shouted into the amulet.

The fairy was reclined on a high mountain ledge, keeping watch on the progress of the travelers through the narrow pass below. He held his own amulet close to his ear but winced and pulled it away as the sorcerer's voice grated through it. "Yes, Master. She is in the mountain pass, but she is not alone. "

"What?" shouted the sorcerer even louder. "Who's with her?" he demanded.

"Some guy. She calls him *Ion*," said the fairy.

"Is it Prince Ion of Beringer?" asked Zimbardo.

"Maybe," replied the fairy sarcastically. "How many guys do you know named Ion?"

"*Ixnay* on the sarcasm, Dash, or I can arrange to have you permanently grounded," he threatened.

As the sorcerer couldn't see him through the amulet, the fairy rolled his eyes. "Yes, Your Evilness," he replied dutifully.

"Describe him. Is he old, bald, and ugly?" the sorcerer inquired hopefully.

"No, more like young, hairy, and handsome. Kind of like a scruffy Prince Charming," reported the fairy.

"Prince Ion!" he exclaimed, frowning. "What's he doing there?"

"I don't know but they make a cute couple," said the tactless fairy.

Zimbardo hissed loudly into his amulet, causing Dash to wince painfully and once more pull the amulet away from his ear. "I am the only Prince Charming worthy of the princess," proclaimed the sorcerer menacingly.

Unseen by Zimbardo, Dash made a sour face and shook his head in disgust.

"The prince has to go!" exclaimed the jealous sorcerer.

"What would you have me do, Oh Nasty One?" inquired the fairy.

"Use *the winged creatures*. Anyway, they owe me a favor," directed the sorcerer.

"Yes, Oh Evil One. I'm on it," said the fairy, stretching languorously on the sunny mountain ledge.

"You'd better be," growled the sorcerer.

After completing a series of leisurely yoga stretches to limber up his small limbs, Dash jumped from the high ledge and swooped down behind the travelers in the mountain pass, being careful to keep a discreet distance. However, Nyx turned around to growl suspiciously in his direction. He'd have to be careful the wolf didn't give him away with his superior sense of smell. Targeting the back of Ion's head, the fairy darted toward him in a sudden blur of wings and pulled out several strands of the boy's dark blond hair.

Nyx barked furiously at the fairy, but he darted away before the humans could see him.

Ion stumbled, almost knocked off his feet. "Ouch!" he shouted, rubbing the back of his head. "What was that?" he asked searching around for the culprit. "It felt like something stung me."

"I don't see any bees...or anything else," said Indigo, looking around them. She turned to Nyx. "Did you see what it was?"

The wolf nodded urgently but alas he could not speak.

"Was it a bee?" she asked him.

The wolf shook his head in frustration.

Ion turned to Bijou. "Did you see anything?" The bat shrugged but zipped off to search the area.

Dash was observing the scene from what he thought was a safe perch high above the travelers on the rocky ledge. He gulped in shock as the large bat rose up unexpectedly in front of him.

Fearing for his life, the much smaller fairy leapt from the ledge, seeking a hiding spot from the pursuing bat.

Bijou's eyes grew wide as he sensed the fairy; however, before he could snatch him, Dash pointed his crystal amulet at him, deflecting the bat's homing radar. To distract him, the fairy kicked open an insect nest on the side of the pass, releasing a stream of angry black and yellow wasps.

Confused and alarmed, Bijou took off after the wasps, which were now zooming down toward the travelers.

Nyx was the first to hear the loud buzzing as it approached them. He growled a warning at Indigo, pointing his muzzle upward at the closing wasps.

Indigo and Ion looked up to see the insect swarm heading directly at them. "Wasps!" shouted Ion. "Run!"

Nyx immediately scooped up Indigo onto his back and tore off through the mountain pass.

Ion screamed and waved his arms as he fled behind them, hoping to ward off the pursuing insects, though he expected, at any moment, to be engulfed by the stinging swarm. Surprised, he realized that the buzzing had abruptly stopped. Slowing, he glanced behind him. Miraculously, the wasps had vanished.

Bijou hove suddenly into view, belching, loudly. Ion looked confused but then remembered that Bijou often dined on insects. The bat rubbed his belly in satisfaction.

Ion wrinkled his nose in distaste, "*bon appetite.*"

The travelers continued on through the narrow mountain pass, which was growing more treacherous and rocky. Indigo scrambled along behind Ion, doing her best to keep up with him, while Nyx continued to trot behind his mistress, keeping his eyes peeled in case the previous offenders should reappear— or some new threat. Indigo's boot slipped suddenly on a rocky patch of ground.

Hearing her cry, Ion whirled around in time to grab her arm and save her from a tumble onto the sharp stones.

Nyx helped steady her on the other side, glaring a bit at the boy. He was used to being Indigo's sole protector and wasn't quite sure what to make of this tall boy and his close attention to his mistress.

Ion continued to hold her arm protectively. "There're a lot of rocks and loose gravel. Maybe I should hang onto you…in case you slip again," he explained, coloring a little. He didn't at all mind an excuse to hold on to her; however, he perceived that she was quite self reliant and might resist his help.

A moment later, she did indeed gently remove her arm from his grasp. "I'm okay," she assured him. "Besides, I have Nyx to hang onto." She patted the wolf's back as he trotted next to her.

The wolf cast Ion a smug look, reminding the boy of his place.

Independent girl, Ion reflected. Even so, he decided he would continue to walk closely beside her in case she did slip again. Hopefully, the wolf wouldn't nip him. "So…" he said, casting a measuring look at

Nyx, who walked on her other side. "Why is it so important to go all the way to the Sacred Well of Acheron?"

"I need the water for a...potion," she said evasively.

"What kind of potion?" he pressed.

"For my cure," she admitted.

"You hope to find a cure for your curse?"

She nodded. "I've been trying to find one my whole life. I've experimented with every possible combination of herbs and potions but, until now, nothing has worked."

"I've heard a lot of stories about the curse," he told her. "But I'm not sure I know what really happened."

She shook her head. "Well, that makes two of us. My father doesn't like to talk about it. All he would tell me is that it was a vengeful sorcerer who cursed our family."

"Do you know who it was?" he asked.

"No, my father never told me. He forbids anyone to speak his name."

"I see..." said Ion, pondering. "I bet Zozimo would know. I'll ask him when we return," he made a note to himself.

"Well," said Indigo. "If this cure works, I won't have to worry about it. Really, I'd rather not know who he is. I want no further part of any sorcery or black magic," she shuddered.

"But don't you want revenge?" asked Ion. "If a sorcerer cursed me, I'd track him down through the Five Kingdoms and make him pay!" he said vehemently.

"No!" she shook her head. "I don't care about revenge. All I want is to be a normal girl—for once in my life."

"So...what is this cure you're talking about?" he asked her.

"I found it in a book," she said. "In fact, I have it right here." She stopped and slung the travel bag from her shoulder. Reaching into the bag, she extracted the ancient leather
volume, opening it to the bookmarked page. She pointed to the top of the page, "There—you can see for yourself."

Ion studied the page. "*A Cure All for Curses*," he read. "Where did you get this from?"

Indigo shrugged. "It just appeared one night. Like magic." she added.

"What do you mean, *like magic*?" he asked, raising his brows.

"I was just sitting in my greenhouse and there was this sudden black smoke and a loud noise. Then I found the book," she explained.

"That doesn't sound suspicious at all," Ion commented sarcastically.

Indigo sighed. "At this point, I'm willing to try anything."

"Have you considered that it might be a *trick*?" he asked her. "What if someone just wants you to think it will work?"

"Why would someone do that?" she asked, a bit ingenuously.

"Why did someone curse you?" he asked pointedly.

Indigo sighed heavily and dropped her head. "I don't even want to think about that. Of course, you could be right. Maybe this is all just a wild goose chase and I'm endangering my life—and yours—for nothing. But I still have to try. Otherwise, I'll never know for sure." She looked at him, hoping he'd understand her awful dilemma.

"I don't know…" Ion frowned at her, shaking his head. "I don't like the sound of this."

* * *

Dash emerged from his hiding place in a small crack on the rock face where he had taken the opportunity to catch a short nap.   Peering down, he spotted the travelers continuing through the pass.   He was relieved to see that Bijou was once more leading the party and too far away to be a threat.   The fairy yawned and stretched and then flew up to the top of the mountain peak where there were a number of very large birds' nests.

The occupants of the nests were dormant and appeared to be slumbering. The only thing Dash could see were their scaly, bronze colored backs, which appeared to be covered over with long, white, oddly human-like hair.

"*Ah-hem!*" Dash cleared his throat loudly, hoping to wake them. When that failed, he tried whistling.

The creatures began to stir and stretch. Very long, sharp black talons appeared, gripping the sides of the nests. Then the creatures lifted their heads to glare at the tiny intruder. One of them gave a terrible snarl and reached out a talon, trying to snag the fairy. Dash managed to dart out of harm's way. "Hey, I come in peace," he told them, holding up his hands. "Zimbardo sent me."

These were no ordinary birds. While their bodies appeared large and bird-like, their faces looked like wizened human women. These were, in fact, the legendary harpies of mythology, and they were not to be messed with. They were huge and menacing, and they could snatch you, body and soul, and carry you off to Hades….or dinner.

"What do you want with us?" squawked the eldest harpy.

Carefully, Dash handed the harpy the strands of hair he had plucked from the boy's head. He pointed down to the mountain pass where Indigo and Ion were just barely visible. "Get rid of the boy but don't harm the girl," directed the fairy.

The harpy nodded its ugly head. "Oh good, fresh meat," she croaked with an awful smile, revealing rotten but still sharp teeth. Her hungry harpy friends rose up squawking from their nests eager to join her for lunch.

"Remember, don't hurt the girl, or Zimbardo will have my head and make you extinct," he cautioned them before giving a small wave and flitting back to his safe perch. This wasn't going to be pretty.

Down in the mountain pass, Indigo and Ion continued to walk together companionably, unaware of their imminent peril. A strange and piercing cawing startled them and it was growing louder…

"What's that awful noise?" asked Indigo, clapping her gauntlets over her ears.

Bijou began darting about frantically.

Nyx howled in pain as the high-pitched cawing assaulted his sensitive ears.

A moment later, the flock of harpies appeared, descending rapidly towards them.

"Run!" shouted Ion, grabbing her arm.

"What *are* they?" Indigo asked, panting as she ran.

"Harpies!" he exclaimed. "They're half bird and half woman and completely deadly. Zozimo warned me about them."

"Now you tell me," she panted, running as fast as she could beside him.

He glanced over his shoulder horrified to see that they were now almost upon them. He turned to the wolf running beside them, "Nyx, take care of her!"

Nodding, the wolf scooped up his mistress and ran off ahead of him. Hoping to buy time for Indigo, Ion turned and stood his ground, bravely confronting the monsters as they descended upon him. Pulling the dagger from his boot, he began swinging wildly at the huge pursuing bird-creatures. But he was no match for their mythic strength. Two of the harpies sunk their talons into his shoulder and slowly began to lift him from the ground. Squirming desperately in their brutal grasp, Ion continued swinging blindly at them with his dagger but could find little purchase on their tough, scaly hides.

Seeing Ion's imminent peril, Indigo cried out in alarm. Leaping from Nyx's back, she raced back to his side, reaching him just as his feet had left the ground. Summoning all of her strength, she leapt up into the air and wrapped her arms around Ion's waist.

"Save yourself!" he protested.

"Shut up! I'm saving you!" Quickly, she worked off one of her gauntlets, letting it fall to the ground. With her bared hand, she reached up carefully, avoiding Ion, and touched the talons of the two harpies that were piercing hs shoulders. Immediately, the harpies shrieked and stalled in midair. Abruptly, they fell, taking Ion and Indigo tumbling back to the ground with them. Fortunately, they had not risen very high.

Even so, Ion landed on his back with a heavy thump, knocking the breath from him. Indigo fell smack on top of him. Fortunately, she remained conscious of her bared hand and held it out so as not to accidentally touch him. Dazed and breathless, they gazed wordlessly into each other's eyes for a long, shocked moment.

"I think you just saved my life," he gasped, gazing up into her deep blue eyes.

"I did what I could," she said modestly, gazing down into his glazed green eyes.

"Thank you…but it was foolish of you to risk your life like that," he scolded her.

"Why? Would you have preferred that I let the harpies carry you off?" she asked with exasperation.

"No…not really," he had to admit, shaking his head. Death by harpy was not a good way to go. "Are they gone?" he asked, rolling his head from side to side.

"Yes, they're gone…at least for now," she told him.

"Are you all right?" he asked her.

"Yes, but you're bleeding." She could see blood seeping from his shoulders where the harpies had pierced him with their sharp talons. Using her gauntleted hand, she gingerly poked the wound, examining it.

"Ouch!" he yelped. "Is it bad?"

"Well, the puncture wound is fairly deep so there's a danger of infection. Fortunately, I have the perfect potion for that." She jumped abruptly to her feet then realized her hand was still bare. "First, I need to find my gauntlet."

Her eyes fell on the black and shriveled carcasses of the dead harpies. They looked like two half-eaten turkeys with charred feathers flapping over their cracked and protruding ribs. Their skin had melted and the awful black goo was seeping from their nose and mouth. Definitely not a pretty sight.

Seeing the grisly fate of their two friends, the other harpies had wisely turned tail, not wanting to meet the fate of their fallen sisters, and returned to the sanctuary of their mountain top lair.

Still dazed, Ion sat up and gazed at the two decimated harpies. "Whoa! You did that?" he asked in stunned amazement.

She turned to face him, waving her bare, discolored fingers at him.

"That's some curse!" he exclaimed, impressed. "I wish I could do that," he said enviously.

Indigo located her missing gauntlet and pulled it back on. "No, you don't. Believe me," she assured him.

Bijou flew down from his hiding place and settled on Ion's injured shoulder. "Ouch!" he winced. Seeing his bloody wound, the bat leapt off his shoulder onto a nearby branch protruding from the rock face. "Thanks for your help, *intrepid leader*," Ion said sarcastically.

The bat folded his wings across his face, embarrassed. In fairness to him, there was nothing he could have done to help. He was no match for the size and strength of the harpies. Besides, the bat reasoned, if he had been killed, the wingless ones would have been left stranded without a guide. Really, he had only been thinking of their welfare when he had hidden out of sight in a small crevice in the side of the pass. A bit annoyed,

71

Bijou pointed with one wing to the passageway ahead of them, urging them onward with the other.

"I think he wants us to get going," said Ion. "And he's right. There's no guarantee they won't come back—or something worse."

"All right. I just need to put some healing salve on those wounds." Indigo glanced around her. "Where's my bag? " She whirled around, searching. "And where's Nyx?" She hadn't seen the wolf since she had leapt from his back to help Ion. Now he was nowhere to be seen. "Bijou, find Nyx," she directed the bat.

Obediently, Bijou flitted off and soon located the wolf, who was lying about twenty yards off on the side of the pass. His eyes were closed and he wasn't moving. The bat waved urgently to Indigo, who dashed to the side of her fallen companion.

"Oh no! Nyx!" She shook him gently. The wolf's eyes flew open and he whimpered at her. Blood oozed from a long scratch on his side. "You're injured!"

Ion hobbled over to join her, holding her bag. "I thought you might need this."

"Oh, thank you!" she exclaimed gratefully, taking the bag and opening it up. "I'd be lost without this." She rummaged inside for the potion. "Now sit down and I'll patch you both up."

Ion lowered himself gingerly next to the stricken wolf and lightly stroked his bloodied fur. "Hang in there, Big Guy." The wolf tolerated his touch reluctantly. After all, his mistress had risked her life to save the annoying boy.

Adeptly, Indigo applied salve to both of Ion's injured shoulders but left the wounds undressed. It was important to leave puncture wounds uncovered so they wouldn't fester. Next, she turned her attention to the wolf. She applied the same salve to all of his scratches, which fortunately were not too deep.

Peevishly, Bijou hung upside down from a branch, waving at her to hurry along. As he was upside down, he was inadvertently pointing in the wrong direction.

"I'm almost done," she chided him. "Just be patient."

The bat sighed and rolled his eyes at her. Patience was not a virtue when killer harpies could return at any moment.

72

Finally satisfied that she had not missed any scratches on either of them, Indigo returned the salve to her bag, closed it up, and got to her feet. "Okay, I'm ready," she declared to the agitated bat.

Ion winced in pain as he rose unsteadily to his feet. Indigo placed a steadying hand on his arm. "Are you sure you're all right to travel?" she asked in concern.

"I'd feel better after a long nap," he admitted, groaning a bit. But Bijou's right. We need to get going." He crossed to retrieve his travel bag at the side of the path and slung it over his shoulder, forgetting his wound. Yelping in pain, he quickly transferred the bag to his hand.

Nyx also staggered a bit as he rose to his feet. "Are you okay?" she observed him, looking worried. To assure her, he whimpered softly and licked her face.

Ion turned to the bat. "Okay, Bijou, get us out of here. We're sitting ducks in this mountain pass."

Led by Bijou, the travelers resumed their journey, moving as fast as they could, which was just a little slower than previously. All of them were anxious to leave the claustrophobic confines of the narrow and treacherous mountain pass. Fortunately, the end was now in sight.

Chapter Six

The Enchanted Forest

Zimbardo's black crystal mirror was working once more, although it remained a bit *glitchy*. He peered through the mirror, observing the travelers as they neared the end of the mountain pass. The sorcerer grew livid with anger upon seeing that Prince Ion was still alive. "Blasted harpies, they failed me!" Before he could see anything else, the crystal mirror glitched again and went dark. "Worthless modern technology!" Raging with frustration, he picked up the malfunctioning mirror and hurtled it across the room, shattering it into a million fragments.

Barely controlling his fury, Zimbardo reached for the crystal amulet around his neck and hissed into it. "Dash, tell me why Prince Ion is still alive...and maybe I'll let you live."

Perched high in a tree, the fairy watched as the travelers emerged wearily from the treacherous mountain pass. "Don't blame me," he said, speaking into his amulet. "Those harpies didn't have a chance. Everything that girl touches dies."

Zimbardo smiled maliciously. "Delightful, isn't she?"

"She's a regular dream date," said the fairy sarcastically.

Zimbardo rubbed his amulet, causing Dash to vibrate with another electric shock. "Don't speak ill of the princess," he said darkly.

"S...s...sorry, Your Awfulness," the fairy apologized shakily.

"All right, I have another idea," the sorcerer said, speaking into his amulet. "Where are they now?"

Dash peered down at the travelers through the tree canopy, checking their progress. "They're about to enter The Enchanted Forest," he reported.

"Perfect," the sorcerer smirked with a devious smile.

Indeed, the travelers had no sooner left the mountain pass behind than they arrived at a signpost that read, *YOU ARE NOW ENTERING THE ENCHANTED FOREST.*

Indigo studied the signpost in disbelief. "Is this some kind of bad joke?"

Bijou shrugged at her and flew off ahead of them into The Enchanted Forest.

"Don't worry," Ion tried to reassure her. "I've never been, but, if I remember Zozimo's stories correctly, The Enchanted Forest is not as bad as The Haunted Forest...I think." Trying to smile encouragingly, he turned and headed off into the forest.

"Well, that's comforting," she said dubiously. Turning to her wolf companion, Indigo absently stroked his head. "What do you think? Should we follow him?"

Nyx sniffed the air and then yipped, as he appeared to catch the scent of something disturbing. Following his nose, he raced into the woods after Ion.

"Nyx, come back!" she called. But the wolf had already disappeared from sight. She sighed in resignation. "Here we go again." Reluctantly, she hurried off after the wolf and entered the mysterious Enchanted Forest. She caught up with Ion and fell into step beside him.

He smiled at her. "Glad you decided to join us."

While The Haunted Forest had been dark and foreboding, The Enchanted Forest was a vibrant green and full of beautiful flowers that seemed to have an almost rosy glow. The birds were singing cheerfully in the trees and the various woodland animals seemed quite friendly. In fact, they were smiling.

"See, I told you it wasn't so bad," Ion flashed her his slightly goofy grin.

"Well…it *seems* nice…" she broke off, uncertainly looking around. "But why are those animals smiling at us?"

He observed a number of rabbits, squirrels, and raccoons, which appeared to be grinning at them from the edge of the forest. "Well, either they're really friendly or they're…"

"*Enchanted*?" she guessed.

Ion shrugged. "Don't worry; they look pretty harmless." They continued on through the woods, smiling back uneasily at the grinning creatures.

* * *

Zimbardo was in his dusty, unkempt library, throwing feathered darts at his Map of the Five Kingdoms. Most of the darts completely missed the target, as his aim was terrible. However, several of them had landed ominously upon The Kingdom of Abaddon. He retrieved the fallen darts and then lifted the crystal amulet to his lips.

"Dash, are you there?" The crystal crackled with static.

The fairy was flying high above the travelers, so that neither the bat nor wolf could catch his scent. He winced as the static buzzed annoyingly through his amulet, causing Zimbardo's voice to keep breaking up.

"I am here, Oh Weird One," replied the fairy.

"It's time to go to . . ." the sorcerer's voice broke up with static, "… Plan B."

"Plan C*?"* asked the fairy.

"Plan B!" shouted the sorcerer impatiently.

Again, Dash could hardly hear him over the static. "Plan D?*"* he guessed.

"Are you deaf, you annoying little flea?" the sorcerer screamed at him. "Forget it! Use your fairy dust! Tie up our annoying friend and feed him to the flowers."

Unfortunately, his crystal amulet continued to break up, distorting the transmission.   "Drop him from the tower?" asked the confused fairy. "What tower?"

"No, no, no, you dimwitted mite! I said *flower* not tower. Feed him to the flowers!"

Finally understanding, Dash spotted a row of tall sunflowers that were growing along the forest path. Removing a small pouch of fairy dust from his robe, he swooped down and liberally sprinkled the dust over the flowers.

Instantly, the yellow sunflowers began to grow taller. Their stalks began to enlarge and crawl over the pathway, heading toward the travelers, who were about twenty yards ahead.

Nyx growled and nudged Indigo, trying to hurry her along. "What is it, Nyx?" She turned to glance at him and gasped as she caught sight of the giant sunflowers, which now appeared to be deliberately and literally *stalking* them.

Ion walked ahead of her, blissfully unaware of the encroaching danger. Hearing her gasp, he whirled around and froze in shock at sight of the pursuing sunflowers. As they watched in horror, each of the giant sunflower heads suddenly grew a large mouth rimmed all around with shark-like teeth.

"Are they enchanted?" whispered Indigo.

"I'm guessing that's a *yes,*" he surmised. "Run!" he shouted. They dashed off as fast as they could, but the giant sunflowers moved even faster.

Nyx scooped Indigo onto his back just as a vining stalk tried to wrap around her ankle. The wolf was able to elude the stalk but not Ion.

Ion took out his dagger and slashed futilely at the thick stalks as they rose up and began to wrap snakelike around his body. His dagger fell to the ground as the twining stalks moved up his body, encasing his arms.

Hearing Ion's cries behind her, Indigo swiveled around on the wolf's back. She was horrified to see that the menacing sunflowers had now almost completely wrapped themselves around his torso. "Stop, Nyx! We've got to help Ion."

The wolf dashed back to the side of the besieged boy. Slipping from his back, she crossed swiftly to Ion, who was now almost completely cocooned by the encircling stalks. A giant sunflower slithered toward Indigo and began wrapping around her legs.

Quickly, she whipped off both gauntlets and let them fall heedlessly to the ground. "You want a piece of me?" she taunted the sunflowers defiantly. "Here!" She held out her bare, discolored hands, inviting them to attack her.

Deliberately, she allowed the stalks to crawl up her body and wrap around her hands. As they did so, the inflated flower heads began to choke and cough. She squeezed the stalks harder with her bare hands until the murderous flowers finally died and dropped away.

No longer able to speak and almost suffocated, Ion was about to become *flower food* as he was being slowly rolled up toward the gaping maw of the giant sunflower head and its terrible guillotine of teeth.

In the nick of time, Indigo grabbed hold of the giant stalk that was binding Ion. Distracted from their prey, the giant sunflower lowered its razor-like mouth toward Indigo, intending to bite off her head!

Summoning all of her strength, she punched the fearsome flower head, being careful to avoid its grinding teeth. The stricken sunflower wheezed like a deflating balloon. The long, yellow petals surrounding its head shriveled up and fell away, while the row of razor-like teeth suddenly erupted with rot and disintegrated. The telltale, hideous black goo seeped from its mouth. As the sunflower crumpled to the ground, Ion was finally released from his constricting bonds.

Triumphantly, Indigo held up her hands, pretending to blow smoke from her fingers. "Don't mess with me!" she shouted, shaking her blackened fists at the remainder of the looming sunflowers. Frightened, they quickly shrunk back to normal size and scuttled away, resuming their usual place at the side of the forest pathway.

Freed from the choking grasp of the stalks, Ion unspooled and rolled free at Indigo's feet. He gazed up at her in shocked amazement.

"Are you okay?" she asked him, noting the red welts that banded his arms and face.

He nodded at her, still too stunned to say much. "That was awesome! You were awesome!"

"Thanks," Indigo said, shrugging. "I have to admit that was rather… satisfying." She didn't approve of violence, but this had been an act of self-defense. Where had this aggressive, new side of her come from, she wondered? Had it always been lurking inside of her, or was it just a byproduct of their extreme circumstances? She wasn't sure. She was just glad that she had been able to save Ion. She would be bereft if anything were to happen to him.

"Hey, are you sure you want to get rid of that curse?" Ion queried, gazing at the shriveled sunflowers. "It has its advantages . . ."

"I'm sure!" Indigo said resolutely.

Without thinking, she bent to offer him her bare hand.

Also unthinking, Ion reached up to take it—

Seeing his imminent peril, Bijou leapt from his perch in a nearby tree and dive-bombed Ion at top speed, knocking him flat onto his back before Indigo could touch him.

"Hey!" shouted Ion, shocked by the seemingly unprovoked attack. "Bijou, what's gotten into you?" he asked the bat, who continued to hover over him protectively.

"He just saved your life," Indigo said in a small, stark voice as she digested the enormity of their near-fatal encounter. She held up her bare, discolored hand. "Still think I should keep that curse?"

Looking ashen, Ion sat up slowly to face her. "Not so much."

Indigo crossed to retrieve her fallen gauntlets and fastened them securely back on. Returning to Ion, she once more offered him her hand. Still shaken by their close call, he hesitated. "It's okay now," she assured him.

"I know that," he said nonchalantly, trying to act like it was no big deal, and that he
hadn't almost just *toasted* himself. He clasped her gauntlet and she pulled him to his feet. He crossed to retrieve his fallen dagger but groaned as he bent over.

"Are you in pain?" asked Indigo, observing him wince as he attempted to straighten up.

"Only when I breathe," he said, rubbing his side. "The important thing is that I *am* still breathing," he added ruefully.

"You might have a broken rib," she told him. "Come on, we'd better fix you up."

"Let me guess," he said. "You have a potion for that."

She nodded, smiling, and took his arm, as he still looked a bit wobbly on his feet.

He turned his head to look over his shoulder. "Is it just me, or is there a *target* on my back?"

Nyx trotted up with a long stick in his mouth, which he presented to the hobbling boy with a grunt.

"What's this, an enchanted snake?" Ion asked warily, as he accepted the gift.

"It's a walking stick, silly," said Indigo. "That's very thoughtful of you, Nyx." She praised the wolf. He nodded his silvery head.

Ion leaned his weight on the stick as he limped along. "Thanks, Nyx. This helps," he said gratefully to the wolf. "Does this mean we're friends now?"

The wolf shrugged indifferently and returned to Indigo's side.

Above them, Bijou flapped his wings impatiently, urging them to move faster.

"Hey, I'm moving as fast as I can, Bijou. We don't all have wings," he told the bat, who glided easily above them immune to the treachery of the forest floor.

High up in the forest canopy safely hidden from the travelers, Dash reclined on the branch of a tall tree, hungrily munching a small yellow fruit. He was just about to take another bite when a worm inched its way out of the fruit. Dash paused, considering the worm and then popped it into his mouth, savoring it.

* * *

An agitated Zimbardo was in his increasingly disordered library, once again throwing darts at his Map of the Five Kingdoms. As usual, most of the darts missed the large map altogether. Sighing, the sorcerer bent to gather up the fallen darts and then approached the map, standing within arm's distance. Deliberately, he stuck a numbered dart into each of the Five Kingdoms, reserving dart number one for the Kingdom of Abaddon. "That's better," he smirked.

Gazing in satisfaction at his newly darted map, Zimbardo raised his amulet to his lips. "Dash, report, what's going on? Is Prince Ion dead?"

Annoyed at the interruption of his snack, Dash wiped his sticky fingers and picked up his amulet. "Prince Ion is….uh…almost dead." he replied.

"What do you mean *almost?*" snapped the sorcerer. "Is he dead or not?"

"Uh . . .that would be a *not*," the fairy reluctantly admitted. Anticipating an angry tirade, he held the amulet away from his ear.

"You little termite! I'll have your wings for this. This is the second time you've failed me," raged the sorcerer.

"But it wasn't my fault," protested the fairy. "The girl saved him again."

"You were supposed to get the princess out of the way," he shouted.

"Are you kidding?" said the fairy. "I'm not getting anywhere near her. She practically murdered the whole forest with her bare hands."

The sorcerer sighed. "Must I do everything myself?" It was so hard to get competent henchmen these days, he reflected glumly. "All right, forget Prince Ion. I'll take care of him later. It's time to go to Plan D."

The sorcerer's amulet was fading out. "Did you say *B*?" asked the fairy.

"D— as in Dash is a dead duck!" shouted the sorcerer.

The fairy gulped. He knew it was dangerous to push Zimbardo too far.
He must do the sorcerer's bidding as long as he wore the amulet—or else.

"Make sure Princess Indigo gets safely to the Sacred Well of Acheron. It's time she mixed up that cure. I've waited long enough."

"Yes, Master," the fairy replied obsequiously. "Your wish is my command."

"Good," growled the sorcerer. "Make sure you remember that. And make sure that nothing happens to the princess…or I'll make sure something happens to you."

Dash grimaced. "I will guard her with my life," he promised.

* * *

The travelers had arrived at a shady bower in the forest. Clearly in pain but trying not to show it, Ion continued to hobble along, leaning heavily on his walking stick.

81

Indigo surveyed the inviting, flower-filled bower. "Bijou, do you think it's safe to stop here?"

Bijou shot off, zipping about to check out the surrounding area.

With the bat out of the way, Dash approached the travelers, hovering in the shadows at the edge of the bower.

Catching the fairy's scent, Nyx silently crept up on the small creature and pounced upon him.

The nimble fairy was able to elude the wolf's paws but still suffered a terrible fright. He hadn't seen the brute coming and it had almost cost him his life! Quickly, he sprinkled fairy dust over the snout of the barking wolf. Then he darted back to safety on his perch at the top of the forest canopy. That had been too close for comfort. His heart was still hammering with adrenaline. He must take more care around the wolf—or get rid of him.

* * *

Indigo ran over to Nyx to inquire what he was chasing after. "What is it? Do you smell something?" she asked, looking about.

Nyx sniffed everywhere as he rifled madly through the bushes, but he had lost the fairy's scent. Frustrated, he shook his head at his mistress.

Bijou returned from his reconnaissance and nodded at Ion.

"Good, Bijou says it's safe to stop here," he told Indigo.

Wincing, Ion slowly lowered himself to the ground and leaned his back against the trunk of a shady tree. He sighed wearily, closing his eyes. "I just need a two minute nap and I'll be good as new."

Eyeing him with concern, Indigo knelt next to him under the tree and opened her travel bag. "I'd better examine you," she told him. "Could you…uh…lift your shirt?" she asked.

Groaning a bit, Ion removed his shirt over his head, revealing a badly bruised chest. Indigo was pleased to see that the puncture wounds from the harpies' talons were healing. But she winced at sight of the new, angry looking bruises.

"Ooh, that looks nasty!" she exclaimed, wrinkling her brow with distress.

He glanced at her, taken aback. "Sorry, I try to stay in shape."

"Your bruises not your ...uh...chest. That looks just...uh...fine," she trailed off, flustered. She glanced away from his chest, which was indeed *fine*, and returned her attention to the task at hand. "Don't worry, I have the perfect potion."

She rummaged in her bag and pulled out a bottle. Opening it, she began to lightly smooth the herbal potion over his bruises, using her gauntlet. Fortunately, the silver mesh was fine enough to allow her some sensation without absorbing the potion.

"That feels better already," he told her. "You have a healing touch."

"Thanks...but only with my armor on." She raised her gauntleted hands. "Ironic, isn't it? I only want to help people and, instead, everything I touch dies." She sighed, closed the bottle, and returned it to her bag. Exhausted, she slumped next to Ion against the tree trunk.

He turned his face to hers as they sat side by side under the tree. He saw that her cheeks were flushed a rosy pink from the afternoon sun and thought she had never looked lovelier. Her very inviting mouth was close enough to kiss . . .if he dared. *Careful*, he told himself. *Don't scare her.*

Taking a deep breath to steady himself, he smiled at her encouragingly. "Don't worry. We'll find your cure and then you'll be the most awesome princess in all the Five Kingdoms—not that you aren't already," he added, smiling at her appreciatively. He flushed as his thoughts strayed back to those full red lips.

"Thanks . . .Ion," she said, shyly returning his smile. Was it her imagination or was he thinking of kissing her? How would she feel if he did? She had never been kissed before, but she didn't think she would mind too much.

Pretending to yawn, Ion lifted his arm, intending to place it casually around her shoulders. Indigo saw his arm approaching her. Was he actually going to kiss her after all?

"Oww!" Ion groaned, dispelling the mood as he suddenly dropped his arm.

"You're still in pain!" she exclaimed with distress.

"Don't worry. It's not so bad...as long as I don't try to lift my arm... or breathe," he winced but gave her a half smile, attempting to make light of it. He adjusted himself against the tree trunk, trying to get more comfortable but couldn't stop another groan from escaping his lips.

"Maybe some speedwell is what you need," said Indigo thoughtfully. She rummaged in her bag again. "Of course, I have everything but that," she announced in frustration.

Bijou suddenly swooped into view and beckoned to her. "Do you know where to find speedwell?" she asked hm.

The bat nodded. "All right, lead the way," she told him, jumping to her feet.

Nyx also jumped to his feet, ready as always to follow his mistress.

"No, Nyx," she said. "Stay here and get some rest with Ion. Bijou will guide me."

Reluctantly, Nyx retreated and curled up next to Ion, even allowing him to stroke his silvery fur.

"Don't go too far," Ion cautioned her. "We're still in The Enchanted Forest, you know. Bijou, keep an eye on her," he instructed the bat.

Bijou nodded at him and then flew off to locate the speedwell.

Indigo hurried along behind the bat, trying to keep up with him.

* * *

From his perch high in the treetop, Dash watched the scene unfold below him. Except for the bat, the girl was alone now, so maybe it was a good time to execute Plan D. Swiftly, he flew down from the treetop and hovered at the edge of the wood, careful to stay out of range of the bat's radar. He observed the girl closely as she roamed further into the woods, following after the bat. He would let her get just a little further from the boy and then he would strike. It would be almost too easy the fairy chuckled.

As the fairy looked on, the bat suddenly pulled up, nodding to a grassy mound a few yards ahead of the girl. She crossed quickly to the grassy mound where she spotted the speedwell plant.

" Good work, Bijou!" she praised the bat. Indigo took a step forward, bending down to pluck the herb when she suddenly lost her footing and began to fall.

"Ahhhhh!" she cried.

Bijou watched in astonishment as Indigo disappeared from sight.

Hovering above the bat, Dash was also in shock. He could hardly believe his eyes. He had been just about to make his move when the silly girl had suddenly vanished. He reproached himself for waiting too long. Now it was too late. The girl was lost or possibly even dead. What in the world was he going to tell Zimbardo?

Chapter Seven

Into the Crystal Cage

Indigo screamed all the way down as she fell through the hole in the earth hidden by overgrown grass. She landed on her back with a thud, knocking the air from her lungs. Fortunately, she had landed on a patch of springy moss, which cushioned her fall. She lay stunned for several moments then slowly opened her eyes and gazed around her. She was astonished to find herself in the middle of an unbelievably gorgeous crystal cavern. It looked as though she had fallen into the center of a brilliant geode as the walls of the cavern were lined with exposed crystals of every imaginable color. Though the hole admitted little sunlight from above, the cavern was, nonetheless, aglow with a soft iridescent light caused by the reflection of the surrounding crystals. Indigo had seldom seen anything so beautiful in her life. As the breath returned to her lungs, she sat up warily, gazing around in awe at the remarkable cavern.

    Carefully, she got to her feet, checking to see if she had broken any bones in her long fall. Fortunately, she had sustained nothing worse than a few bruises and scratches. Still dazed, she stood a moment, gazing at the glittering crystal cavern, unthinking of anything other than the beauty that surrounded her.

She was startled out of her trance by the sudden appearance of Bijou, who zoomed down the hole and hovered in front of her face. "Bijou!" she exclaimed in surprise. "Where am I?"

The bat put a webbed finger to his lips, warning her to be quiet. Then he pointed urgently at something behind her.

Before Indigo could turn around, she heard a terrible rattling and scraping sound that sent fear coursing through her. Whirling around, she was horrified to see what appeared to be a giant, slumbering dragon. The rattling had come from a massive chain that was coiled around its neck. The dragon was moving restively in its sleep, causing the chain to rattle.

Indigo caught her breath as she stared at the huge, slumbering beast. Clearly, this was no ordinary dragon with scaly green lizard skin. Instead, this creature looked as if it had been forged from the crystalline walls of the cavern. Its skin was almost translucent and gleamed with a purplish glow. In place of ugly scales, it had rows of beautiful amethyst crystals.

Indigo gasped in terror as the dragon opened one large golden eye to stare at her. "Bijou, help me!" she whispered.

Equally alarmed, the bat grasped hold of her arms and attempted mightily to lift her from the ground. Fiercely, he fluttered his small webbed wings and, summoning all of his strength, struggled to hoist her into the air. Slowly, Indigo's feet began to lift from the ground. Unfortunately, the bat was simply not large enough to raise her up more than a few inches. Despite his best efforts, he lost his grip on the much larger girl, causing Indigo to tumble back to the ground with an involuntary cry.

Immediately, the dragon's other golden eye popped open. Indigo froze in horror as the creature calmly surveyed her from head to toe, moving only its eyes. A feeling of sick dread filled Indigo as she realized that she was stranded in the cavern at the mercy of this giant creature.

Desperate, she turned back to the hovering bat. "Bijou, get help! Hurry!" she implored him.

Nodding at her, the bat zoomed back up the hole.

Now fully awake, the dragon rose slowly to its feet, rattling the restraining chains around its neck.

Terrified, Indigo spotted a large boulder at the side of the cavern and ran to crouch behind it, hoping the chained monster could not reach her there.

The dragon rose to its full, frightening height and unfurled its huge, amethyst colored wings. Then it roared loudly, spewing a stream of fire in Indigo's direction. The fire struck the boulder she was crouched behind but fortunately did not reach her. Shaking with fear, Indigo attempted to roll herself up into a small ball behind the boulder.

Frustrated that it could not reach her, the dragon roared again and leapt forward, straining futilely against its chains. It spewed another stream of fire in the girl's direction.

This time the dragon's fire caught the hem of Indigo's lavender gown. Gasping with horror, she managed to beat out the flame before it could ignite her dress. Still crouched behind the large rock, she lifted the corner of her dress, revealing a white petticoat beneath. Quickly, she tore off a piece of the petticoat and tied it to a nearby stick.

She stuck out the makeshift white flag and waved it at the dragon. *"Cease fire?"* she called tremulously.

"Who dares to enter my chamber?" the dragon roared in a baritone, yet feminine, rumble.

Cautiously, Indigo poked her head around the corner of the boulder. "It's me, Princess Indigo of Abaddon. I mean you no harm. And you are …?" she inquired boldly.

"I am the Great Crystal Dragon, Narli. I have been imprisoned here for years by your kind and forgotten." The dragon sniffed in her direction. "You smell funny…like death."

"It's my curse," said Indigo. "I kill things."

To demonstrate, she pulled off one of her gauntlets and touched a nearby bush that was growing near the boulder. The small bush instantly disintegrated.

Startled, Narli roared and took a step back from her. "You are a sorceress?" she asked suspiciously.

"No, it's just a curse. I can't control it," explained Indigo.

"Perhaps I should kill you?" considered the dragon.

"No, don't do that!" exclaimed Indigo. "I promise you I mean you no harm. I'm trying to find the Sacred Well of Acheron so I can remove the curse."

The dragon snorted skeptically. "How do you intend to get past the Great Serpent?

"I don't know," Indigo admitted. "I haven't figured that part out yet."

"It will eat you!" exclaimed the dragon with unnerving certainty.

"Any ideas on that?" asked Indigo, wincing.

"You must give it something of equal value to the sacred water," the dragon explained.

"Like what?" said Indigo. Hopefully, if she could keep the conversation going long enough, the volatile creature would forget to incinerate her.

Narli lifted a wing, revealing a beautiful shiny stone about the size of an ostrich egg. "You must give it a Serpent Stone."

"Great!" said Indigo as she stood up and started toward the stone.

Narli roared and dropped her wing back over the stone. "Not so fast! If you want the stone, you must first free me." She shook her huge head, rattling the chain around her neck.

"Okay…" said Indigo, uncertain if that was really a good idea or not. "Do you…uh…have a key?"

"The key is on the other side of the cavern…over the crevasse," the dragon added.

"Crevasse?" asked Indigo. She didn't at all like the sound of that.

* * *

Meanwhile, Bijou had retrieved Ion and Nyx and led them back to the grassy mound where Indigo had disappeared. Warning them both to approach with caution, he pointed to the largely hidden hole in the ground, which was about three feet wide and covered over by long grass.

Dash hovered out of sight above them, also desperate to learn of Indigo's fate. He knew that Zimbardo would not hesitate to kill him (as painfully as possible) if he failed in his mission to safely deliver the princess to him.

Ion moved aside the grass, revealing the gaping hole in the ground. "She's down there?" he asked, horrified.

Bijou nodded urgently.

"I thought you were watching her?" he scolded him.

The bat shrugged helplessly.

"All right…it's not your fault.   You probably didn't see the hole under all this grass."

The bat nodded at him glumly.

Ion fell flat on his belly and peered over the edge of the deep hole. "I don't see anything," he said.   "Indigo, can you hear me?" he shouted into the hole.

Below him in the cavern, Indigo was relieved to hear Ion's voice.

"Who's that?" asked Narli suspiciously.

"It's Prince Ion of Beringer. He's helping me find the cure."

The dragon snorted skeptically.

Indigo stood directly under the hole and waved her arms wildly. "Ion! I'm down here!" she shouted.

"I see you!" he shouted, waving back at her. "Don't worry. I'm going to get you out of there."   Removing the dagger from his boot, he crossed to the nearby woods and cut a long length of thick vine. "You'd better not be *enchanted,"* he muttered. Fortunately, the vine did not answer back and remained limp in his hands.

He lashed one end of the long vine over a sturdy tree then crossed back to the hole where he dropped the rest of the vine over the side. "Hold on, Indigo! I'm coming," he shouted down the hole.

Above him, unseen, Dash was poised to dart down the hole after Ion.   He must find out what had become of the girl. His life depended upon her survival.

Ion had no sooner lowered himself over the edge of the hole than a column of flame leapt up from below, singing his posterior.

"Ahhhh!" he screamed, scrambling back to safety at the top of the hole and rubbing his backside. "What the hell was that?" he shouted down to her.

Above him, Dash was also frantically beating out a flame that had singed his wings as he had attempted to follow Ion over the edge.

"Don't worry. It' s just a dragon," Indigo called up to Ion.

"Just a dragon?!" he said incredulously.

Above him, Dash rolled his eyes in equal disbelief.

"It's okay. Her name is Narli. She's an enchanted crystal dragon, and she's actually quite lovely. She's chained up…and we've made a deal," she informed him.

" A deal? You can't make a deal with a dragon. They're not trustworthy,"Ion shouted back at her. From down below he could hear the dragon roar in protest. "No offense."

"Don't worry, I can handle this," Indigo yelled back at him.

"Maybe…but I'm coming down anyway," he declared. He grasped the vine and again lowered himself over the edge of the hole.

This time, Dash decided not to follow the boy. He was glad of his decision when another a column of fire streamed up to greet Ion. Yelping, he scrambled back out of the hole.

Hovering above him, Dash shook his head glumly. There was no way he was going down that hole. He could not risk being *flambéed* by the dragon.

"Sorry, Narli doesn't seem to trust you," Indigo shouted up to Ion.

"Oh, how ironic! The dragon doesn't trust me!" he said sarcastically. He stuck his face over the hole. "Well, the feeling is mutual because I sure as hell don't trust her!"

Narli blew a stream of smoke up into Ion's face, causing him to choke.

Above him, Dash also got caught in the stream of smoke. As he was so tiny, he was easily overcome and almost asphyxiated by the foul fumes.

"You're not helping, Ion. Trust me, okay? I have a good feeling about this," Indigo assured him, perhaps a bit naively.

"Famous last words," Ion muttered to himself. Shaking his head, he reluctantly called down to her. "All right, have it your way, but I don't like it. I'm here if you need me." He assumed a fighting stance at the side of the hole. He would do whatever he must to protect her, even if it meant wrestling a *crystal dragon*.

Indigo turned back to Narli, shaking her head apologetically. "Men! They're always trying to rescue you."

Narli chuckled in amused agreement.

"So, we have a deal. If I get the key and free you, then you'll give me the Serpent's Stone?" asked Indigo hopefully.

Narli nodded in agreement and pointed the way with her large, purple wing. "It's that way. Stay close to the wall and whatever you do, don't fall," she cautioned her. "You're not the first to try this," she added ominously.

Following Narli's wing, Indigo moved off cautiously toward the rear of the cavern where the crevasse began. It was a deep fissure in the earth about ten feet across. A very narrow ledge edged along one side of the crevasse—barely wide enough for her to walk on. Fortunately, it was not entirely dark as some light filtered from above and through cracks in the rock wall. Still, it would be a very treacherous endeavor—with poor odds of success.

Questioningly, Indigo turned back to look at Narli. "Are you sure the key is back here?"

The dragon nodded at her, motioning for her to continue.

Indigo peered over the side of the steep crevasse but could not see the bottom. Something gleamed white below her. She gasped as she realized it was a number of splayed and fractured human skeletons. They had been impaled on the spiky rock fingers lining the crevasse. Narli had told the truth. She was clearly not the first to attempt to retrieve the key. She gulped, hoping she would not meet the same fate as her unfortunate predecessors.

* * *

Back on his safe perch high in the forest canopy, Dash lay prone on a large leaf, trying to recover himself. That was his first encounter with a dragon and he hoped it would be his last! Fortunately, his wings were not so badly damaged that he couldn't fly. However, his lungs felt seared by the smoke and it was hard for him to speak without coughing. As he lay, gasping and trying to catch his breath, the crystal amulet around his neck began to vibrate. Reluctantly, he picked it up. "Yes?" he coughed.

"Dash, is that you?" Zimbardo's voice crackled over the amulet. He was pacing nervously in his library. The fairy was overdue to check in and he feared the worst. "Report! What's going on with the princess? Is she safe?"

"Y...yes, Master," he croaked. "I am keeping a...cough...close...
cough...watch on her."

"What's wrong with you?" snapped the sorcerer. "Stop coughing in
my ear!"

"Sorry, I think I'm...*cough*...allergic to...cough...smoke," wheezed
the fairy.

"*Smoke?*" snapped the sorcerer. What smoke? Is the princess in
danger?"

"Sorry, you're...*cough*...breaking up..." Deliberately, the fairy
smacked his fist on the amulet, simulating loud static.

Wincing, Zimbardo held the amulet away his ear and shouted into it.
"If you fail me, I'll have your wings mounted in my library!" Disgusted, he
let the amulet fall back around his neck and resumed pacing—passing by
several pairs of fairy wings already mounted on the adjacent wall.

Distressed by the sorcerer's threat, Dash curled up into a fetal position
on the leaf, "I...*cough*...hate that guy!"

* * *

Down in the crystal cavern, Indigo was also trying to calm herself as she
prepared to traverse the deep crevasse. Taking a deep breath, she stepped
out onto the narrow ledge and began to very slowly edge herself along it.
The ledge was not quite as wide as her feet, so she had to move along it in
sideways fashion like a crab. At one point her foot slipped suddenly on a
patch of loose pebbles. Fortunately, she was able to catch herself before she
plunged over the side into oblivion—or was impaled on the sharp rocks
below.

For a panicked moment, she clung onto the rock wall like a bat,
breathing heavily. When she felt calmer, she looked down and located the
loose stones. Carefully, she brushed them from the ledge with her boot.

She resumed inching her way sideways along the narrow ledge. Then
she saw it! A large gold key gleamed at her in the near distance. She only
had a little further to go and it would be hers. Encouraged, she inched
along a little faster, keeping her eyes on the glittering prize. Suddenly, her
left foot stepped into the air—

Gasping in shock, she froze and looked down. There was a break in the pathway! Regaining her balance, she retracted her foot from empty space and placed it securely back on the ledge. If she had been going any faster, she would certainly have fallen to her doom.   The break extended about two feet across where the ledge resumed once more. If she wanted the key, she would have to somehow cross the break to reach it. A long board would have been nice to bridge the gap, but that was unfortunately not a possibility. Gulping, she realized that her only option was to leap across the break.   Normally, it would be easy for her to leap across such a short distance. The tricky part would be landing, as it appeared to be even narrower on the other side of the break.

I can do this! I can do this! she thought, giving herself a pep talk. Taking a deep breath, she leapt nimbly across the break in the ledge, landing with the grace of a dancer. The key was now only a foot away from her. Quickly, she edged her way toward it and seized it! But she could not pull it away. She wiggled it carefully trying to dislodge it from its bed on the rock wall. But it would not budge.   Grimacing, she realized it was stuck. Now what?

She looked around her, searching for something she might use as a tool. She spotted a rock the size of her palm, lying not too far from her feet. She stooped carefully to pick it up. Grasping the stone she smashed it against the rock that encircled the key. She was gratified when some of the rock enclosure began to crumble away. She hammered even harder and the key slipped free!   Gasping, she reached down and somehow managed to catch the key before it was lost forever at the bottom of the crevasse.

Her relief turned to panic as the ledge beneath her feet suddenly started to crack. Her hammering on the stone must have triggered a deeper break than she thought. Squeezing the key tightly in her gauntlet, she hurriedly leapt back across the break.

As Indigo landed on the other side, she turned to glance behind her. Shocked, she saw that the ledge she had previously stood upon had now crumbled away completely.   As adrenaline shot through her body, she quickly scooted her way along the ledge back to the relative safety of the crystal cavern.

Narli was anxiously waiting for her return. Spotting the dragon, Indigo waved the key at her. "I've got it!" she shouted triumphantly.

"Unlock me, quickly!" demanded the dragon.

Indigo pulled up, panting, just short of the waiting dragon. "Wait a minute! I just risked my life for this key. How do I know you won't double-cross me?"

"Dragon's honor?" Narli shrugged.

Indigo looked at her dubiously. "What else?" she asked.

"Because I'm beautiful?" Narli batted her long eyelashes at her and flashed light through her amethyst crystal scales. She really was a magnificent creature.

But Indigo frowned at her unconvinced. "That's a bit superficial. I need something a little more substantial before I can unlock you," she waved the key at her enticingly.

"Sorry, I'm used to dealing with men, " Narli apologized. "In return for my freedom, I will aid you on your quest and take you to the well," she promised solemnly.

"That's better," she nodded at the dragon, still not entirely convinced. She could only hope that the dragon would honor their bargain. Holding the key aloft, she slowly crossed to the captive beast. Narli knelt down and lifted her head out of the way so that she would not accidentally breathe smoke or fire on the fragile girl.

Warily, Indigo leaned upon the dragon's long neck and carefully fitted the key into the lock. She turned it but nothing happened. She turned the key again and again without luck.

"Well, I'm waiting," said Narli impatiently.

"Sorry, I'm trying but it won't open," Indigo cried.

"This better not be a trick…" the dragon warned.

Desperate, Indigo tried repeatedly to turn the key in the lock but it refused to turn. "Really, I'm trying as hard as I can, but it doesn't seem to work," she assured the glowering dragon. "Are you sure it's the correct key?" She hated to think she had risked her life for nothing.

Narli lifted her head and roared in frustration. Startled, Indigo dropped the key, which fell at the dragon's feet. The dragon examined the key. "It looks a bit rusty," she observed. "Stand away!" she ordered the girl. She pointed with her wing, "Go behind the rock."

Indigo scrambled to safety behind the large boulder and crouched behind it. She poked her head out, curious to see what the dragon would do.

"Keep your head down," the dragon cautioned her. Taking a deep breath, the dragon issued a stream of boiling hot steam at the key. Instantly, the rust dissolved, leaving the golden key looking bright and shiny. "Try it now," ordered Narli.

Indigo approached the dragon once more and bent to pick up the key. "Wow, it looks like new," she said, eyeing the gleaming key.

"Careful, it might still be hot," the dragon cautioned her.

Tentatively, Indigo touched the key. Fortunately, her silver gauntlet protected her hand from a burn, but even through the silver mesh, she could feel that it was still quite warm. Clutching the key in the palm of her gauntlet, she turned again to face the dragon. As before, Narli obligingly lifted her head so that the girl could safely reach the lock.   Taking a deep breath, Indigo again inserted the key into the lock around the dragon's neck.

Taking another breath, she slowly turned it. And the lock sprang open!

With a victorious snort, Narli shook her head free of the chains and unfurled her crystal wings to their full span. Light flashed brilliantly throughout the length of her body, and bounced off the exquisitely colored crystal walls, creating an amazing light display.

Indigo jumped back in alarm as the freed dragon now towered above her threateningly. "Don't forget we have a deal," she said in a small voice. At that moment, she wasn't at all sure that the dragon would honor her word. After all, she hadn't heard too many nice things about dragons.

Narli beamed down happily at the trembling girl. "A promise is a promise," she said. With that, she used her tail to push the shiny Serpent Stone toward her.

Keeping a watchful eye on the dragon, Indigo approached slowly and scooped up the shining Stone. "Thank you," she said. "Are you sure this will work on the Serpent of Minerva?"

The dragon nodded thoughtfully. "Works like a charm. All the same, he's the touchy sort, so I wouldn't get on his bad side, if I were you."

"I'll try not to," Indigo nodded, clutching the precious Stone with both hands.

She glanced around her at a sudden loss. "Uh...how do I get out of here?"

"Come on," said the dragon, "It's high time to blow this crystal cage." So saying, she extended her long neck toward the girl. "Hop on! Hang on tight and stay low!" she commanded.

Obediently, Indigo climbed gingerly onto the dragon's back and leaned forward, tightly gripping onto the amethyst scales around Narli's neck.

With a mighty leap, the dragon flew upward and, with tremendous force, rocketed up out of the hole with Indigo clinging tightly to her back.

Still standing in attention at the side of the hole in case Indigo should call to him, Ion was knocked backwards in shock as the dragon shot up out of the hole. Along with Bijou and Nyx, he watched in stunned amazement as Narli soared overhead, making joyful loops in the air as Indigo clung to her back.

As Narli leveled out, Indigo released her urgent grip on the dragon's neck and sat upright, gazing down at her friends, who appeared very small below her. At first, she had been frightened, but as she relaxed, she realized she was having fun. After all, it wasn't everyday a girl got to fly on the back of a dragon. She waved jubilantly at her friends.

"Indigo?!" Ion gasped in dazed disbelief as he saw her waving down at him.

Nyx pointed his muzzle upward at the dragon and howled mournfully, worried that he had permanently lost his beloved mistress.

Bijou shot high into the sky, trying to catch up with the dragon. Finally, he pulled alongside of Indigo, being careful to avoid the dragon's head.

Indigo waved at him, "Don't worry, I'm fine!" she shouted cheerfully at him.

Narli suddenly sped up, causing the much smaller Bijou to tumble backwards as he got caught in the dragon's backwash. The bat righted itself in the air and flapped off, attempting to once more catch up with the giant creature.

As Ion watched nervously, the flying dragon suddenly lowered its head and now appeared to be zooming straight at him. Beside him, Nyx howled fiercely. Both of them scrambled backwards desperately as the huge dragon loomed closer and closer to them until it was almost directly above them. Wincing, Ion closed his eyes, bracing for impact. He felt a long *whoosh* of air pass over him. When he opened his eyes, he saw that the dragon had executed a perfect landing about three feet in front of him.

Indigo smiled brightly at Ion and scooted forward on the dragon's long neck. "Hop aboard!" she said. "We're getting a lift."

A bit shakily, Ion approached the side of the crouching dragon. Secretly, he was debating whether or not to pull his dagger when Narli suddenly craned her head around and looked him straight in the eye.

"Welcome aboard," she greeted him.

"Hey there," Ion replied, taken aback by the creature's apparent friendliness.   Maybe he would keep his dagger sheathed after all.

Uncertainly, he climbed onto the dragon's back behind Indigo. "Are you sure about this?" he muttered to her.

"No," she whispered back. "But do you have a better idea?"

He shrugged at her and then leaned forward, wrapping his arms securely around her waist and laying his head on her shoulder. Oh well, he thought, there were less pleasant ways to die.

"You, too, Nyx!" she called to the wolf.   "Hop on!"

Looking very reluctant, the wolf leapt onto the dragon's back behind Ion and wrapped his forepaws around his waist. Deliberately, he dropped his large muzzle onto the boy's shoulder, which was still tender from the harpies' piercing talons.   Wincing, Ion turned his head and locked eyes with the wolf. Getting the message, Nyx lifted his head from Ion's shoulder but still laid most of his ample weight on his back, causing a bolt of pain to shoot through the boy's injured rib.

Ion thought he could not be more uncomfortable until Bijou suddenly hopped up and perched on his other injured shoulder. Ion turned his head to look at the bat, *"Really?"* he asked.

The bat shrugged.   He knew the dragon could fly much faster than he could, and he couldn't afford to lose them.

 It was going to be a long flight, reflected Ion.

"Hold on!" ordered Narli as she rose up into the air and flew off over the horizon.

* * *

Flying far behind, Dash tried hard to keep the dragon in sight. He couldn't believe that the girl had survived her ordeal and was now flying on the back of the dragon! Maybe it wasn't too late, after all, to execute *Plan D*...

Chapter Eight

The Belly of the Beast

The four travelers flew for almost an hour on the dragon's back. Indigo continued to enjoy her unexpected airborne journey though they flew over an uninviting vista below, including what looked like a large swamp area covered over with a dark cloud of swarming insects. It was a good thing they were getting a lift she thought, as it would have been most unpleasant to walk through such *buggy* terrain.

Seated behind her on the dragon's back, Ion would have enjoyed the flight a lot more if the wolf and bat hadn't been literally riding on his sore shoulders. Fortunately, Bijou didn't weigh much, but the wolf was quite heavy and breathed down his neck the entire time, scratching him more than once with his claws.

Nyx couldn't help it. He was having a terrible time trying to stay balanced on the dragon's back. Several times he had almost slipped off. It wasn't his fault that he had to repeatedly claw at the boy's head and back in order to avoid falling.

Fortunately, Narli flew in a largely straight flight pattern and made few sharp turns.

Along the way, the dragon kept Indigo updated on their progress, along with some rambling, in-flight commentary on the general uselessness of humans, their over poaching of dragons, and the urgent need to place her species on the endangered list before it was too late. Indigo assured Narli that when she returned to court, she would do her best to lobby the king on behalf of her and her winged brethren.

About ten minutes later, as they were flying over a dense forest, Narli turned her long neck once more to speak to Indigo. "This is as far as I go. Ahead lies the Valley of Vervain." Lowering her head, the dragon swooped down and executed another smooth landing, coming to rest on a rugged hill, overlooking the wide, green valley below.

The travelers slid gratefully off the dragon's back happy to once more be on solid ground. Indigo looked remarkably fresh, but Ion wobbled about stiffly and looked the worse for wear. His shaggy blonde hair was badly mussed, and his shirt was ripped in several places thanks to the wolf's repeated pawing at him during the flight.

Nyx wobbled about even worse than Ion, and it took him some moments to recover his equilibrium. Seeing his distress, Indigo dropped to her knees beside her faithful companion, wrapped her arms about his shaggy neck, and kissed his head soothingly.   "Poor, Nyx, are you all right? I know you're not used to flying."

The wolf whimpered, glad to have a little sympathy.

Almost in tatters, Ion looked indignantly at the pair. "Hey, what about me? Your little wolfie almost *shredded* me!" He pointed to the scratches on his arms and face.

However, this information seemed only to increase Indigo's concern for the wolf. "Oh you poor boy, you must have had a dreadful time."

The wolf nodded, whimpering a little more. She gave his head another kiss.

Ion could have sworn that the wolf was smirking at him. Exasperated, he turned away from the cozy pair and scanned the fertile green valley that lay before them.

He turned back to Narli, who was catching her breath before taking off once more. "So that's the Valley of Vervain. Are we near the Sacred Well of Acheron?"

The dragon nodded and pointed her wing at about two o'clock. "Once you get beyond that ridge of trees, you'll see the Sacred Well."

"All right," said Ion, turning back to Indigo. "I suggest we get going while we still have daylight." The late afternoon shadows were already growing long.

Indigo rose to her feet and crossed to give Narli an appreciative hug around the neck. "Thanks for the ride, Narli. I hope you enjoy your freedom."

Narli expressed her jubilance by flashing light through her crystal scales. "I will," she said as she crouched low in preparation for take off. "And I hope you find your cure. Remember the Serpent Stone—and your promise."

"I will," Indigo assured her.

With that Narli lifted off and flew a figure eight over the travelers. Dipping a wing at them, she called out, "Good luck! You'll need it!"

The pair waved back, watching as the dragon disappeared into the distance. Frowning, Ion turned to face Indigo. "Do you think she knows something we don't?"

"Don't worry, we have the Serpent Stone..." she assured him.

"If it works..." he muttered, darkly.

"It'll work!" Indigo assured him. "I hope..." They exchanged a rueful glance.

"Well, there's only one way to find out," said Ion. "Let's go!" He glanced around, suddenly realizing that one of their traveling party was missing. "Hey, where's Bijou?"

Looking around, they spotted the bat swinging by his feet in a nearby tree. Ion whistled softly to get his attention. Reluctantly, the bat flew down from the tree and hovered in front of them. He was still a bit dizzy from the flight, as he was not used to such speed.

"Sorry to disturb your nap, but I thought you were leading this expedition."

The bat shrugged at him in annoyance. After all, he was entitled to a short *bat break*.

"We need to get to the Sacred Well before the sun goes down. You've been there before, right?" Ion queried him.

The bat nodded and pointed in the same direction that Narli had previously indicated. In order to reach the valley below them, they would first have to negotiate their way down the steep hill that lay before them.

Impatiently, Bijou motioned them forward and zipped off, flying down the rugged hillside, though of course it was much easier to fly over the steep hillside than to walk down it.

Nyx bounded eagerly after the bat, as it was also easier to trot on four legs than walk on two.

The bat pulled up and doubled back to wait for his land-bound charges.

Indigo regarded the steep slope with dismay. "I wonder why Narli didn't take us into the Valley?"

Ion snorted skeptically. "Maybe she was afraid to." He held out his hand to her. "You'd better let me help you down. This looks a bit treacherous."

This time, Indigo did not dissent and gladly took hold of his offered hand. Carefully, they began their descent down the steep slope, which was covered with large rocks and full of unspecified rodent holes.

"Mind the burrows," he cautioned her.

They were about half way down the slope, when a hideous looking little beast suddenly popped out of a burrow in front of her, badly startling Indigo.

"Aaaah!" she shrieked. She stepped backwards, losing her balance in the process. If Ion had not been holding her hand, she surely would have taken a bad tumble.

Hearing her distressed cry, Nyx dashed back up the hill and chased off the offending beast, who quickly disappeared down another hole.

"W-was that a r-rat?" she quivered. She really, really did not like rats!

Ion could feel her trembling, so he pulled her into his arms to soothe her. "Don't worry. I'm pretty sure it was just a *burgo*. They're ugly as hell but usually harmless. "Are you okay?"

She grimaced, lifting her foot. "My ankle hurts a little but I don't think it's sprained. Fortunately, I have a potion for that."

"I'm sure you do," he said amused.   He was beginning to think she had more potions than Zozimo.   "Do I need to carry you again?"

"Don't be silly," she chided him. "I just need a little help, so I don't put too much weight on my ankle."

Obligingly, he wrapped a steadying arm around her back and held her close. She leaned against him as they continued their descent.

Truthfully, her ankle was feeling a lot better, but she was glad to feel his strong arm around her. It made her feel a little braver and more confident as they continued down the daunting hill toward the Sacred Well…and the Serpent!

Finally, they reached the bottom of the hill and set off through the level grassland, following Bijou's lead. They had gone about half a mile when the bat flitted ahead of them some fifty yards. Hovering, he pointed urgently to something that lay below him.

"Come on! I think Bijou has found the well!" shouted Ion.

They ran forward until they could see that the bat was indeed hovering over a small, round, topless well that was made of smooth gray stones.

"That's it?" asked Indigo in surprise. "It looks quite small and ordinary. Not much like a *sacred* well." She started forward but Ion grabbed her by the arm, stopping her.

"Wait a minute. What about the serpent?" he asked her warily.

They both stared ahead at the small well, searching for any telltale signs of the giant reptile, but there were none to be found

"I don't see any serpent, do you?" Indigo asked him

"No…" he replied tentatively, "Either it's our lucky day…or it's hiding…"

"Hiding?" repeated Indigo worriedly. "Where do you think it would hide?"

They scanned the perimeter around the well, including the surrounding woods but again saw nothing out of the ordinary. Ion shrugged. "It could be anywhere…maybe even in the well…"

"Hmm," she pondered. "You could be right about that. Maybe we should look inside." She started forward again, but once more Ion restrained her.

"Wait! It's too dangerous. What if it's lurking inside and shoots up and grabs you?"

Indigo sighed heavily. "Well, we can't just stand here, can we?" she asked a bit exasperated. "Do *you* want to look?"

"Not particularly," he admitted.

They both turned to look expectantly at Nyx, but the silver wolf backed away, grimly shaking his head at them.

Just then Bijou flew back to them, trying to urge them forward.

"Bijou, do you know where the serpent is?" Ion asked him.

The bat shrugged, shaking his head.

"Do you think it could be hiding inside the well?" he asked.

The bat shrugged again as if to say *possibly.*

"Would you be willing to look inside the well?" he queried hopefully.

The bat considered a long moment, before nodding in the affirmative.

"Good," said Ion. "If there's any trouble, you can move a lot faster than we can. Just be careful, okay?"

The bat nodded again and then flew off toward the well. He hovered for a moment over the top before dipping down and disappearing inside.

Indigo and Ion waited anxiously for the bat's return. One minute elapsed and then another. They exchanged uneasy glances. After five minutes they were really getting nervous.

"He's been down there an awful long time," said Indigo. "Do you think something happened to him?"

Ion sighed worriedly. "I hope not." He cupped his hands around his mouth and called out, "Bijou, come back!"

Still the bat did not return. Ion pulled the dagger from his boot and turned to Indigo. "You wait here. I'm going to look in the well."

"No way! I'm coming, too," she told him. "Remember, I have the Serpent Stone." She opened her bag and pulled out the Stone.

"All right," he said. "Just stay behind me, okay?"

She nodded and together they slowly approached the well. Indigo followed closely behind Ion, clutching the Stone to her chest. They reached the side of the well and Ion bent over warily to peer inside.

"Bijou!" he called down the well. "Can you hear me?" But there was no response. He turned back to Indigo. "It's too dark. I can't see anything," he told her.

"Now what?" she asked. "How am I going to get any water?"

Ion considered her options. "Well, if you have an empty bottle I might be able to find a long vine. Maybe I can tie it around the bottle and lower it into the well…"

"Okay, it's worth a try," she said. She opened her bag and began rummaging inside for an appropriate bottle.

As she did so, the ground beneath them began to rumble and shake alarmingly. Terrified, they stared at each other. "What's that?" she cried, swaying with the motion.

"Feels like an earthquake," he said, trying to stay upright. As she staggered, he grabbed hold of her, "Hang onto me!" he yelled.

Nyx howled furiously, sniffing at the rumbling well.

Indigo and Ion clung to each other in fear as the shaking grew worse. A moment later, a huge serpent burst up from the well. It towered over them, baring long, sharp fangs!

"I am the Serpent of Minerva, guardian of the Sacred Well of Acheron. You have trespassed and now you must die!" roared the monstrous beast.

They froze in terror as the serpent bent its giant head threateningly toward them, stretching its mouth wide. As it did so, Bijou suddenly shot up out of its gullet. He appeared slimy and dazed but otherwise unhurt.

"Bijou!" cried Ion in shocked surprise.

Momentarily distracted, the serpent turned his large head away from them, trying to recapture the escaped bat. Fortunately, Bijou was able to dart away to safety before the creature could swallow him up again.

"The Stone, the Stone!" Ion shouted to Indigo. "Give him the Stone, quickly!"

Indigo's hands were shaking so badly that she accidentally dropped the Serpent Stone, which rolled rapidly away from her. Crying out, she raced to retrieve it.

"Indigo, watch out!" shouted Ion as he stepped between her and the threatening serpent, raising his dagger.

Clutching the Stone, Indigo whirled around and froze in terror. The scaly green head of the giant serpent was now hovering immediately in front of her. Its glowing amber eyes coolly appraised her.

"Show me the Stone!" he roared at her.

Indigo backed up in terror as Ion leapt in front of her, bravely brandishing his dagger at the looming serpent.

Displeased, the creature hissed loudly at them. Then he stretched his mouth wide enough to engulf both of them, revealing rows of needle-sharp teeth.

"Wait! I'll give you the Stone. I brought it for you." She jumped forward, clutching the Stone tightly between her gauntlets, and thrust it upward at the menacing serpent.

The serpent paused considering her offering. Its mouth was now just inches from her face. She wrinkled her nose as its hot, fetid breath washed over her. "Where did you get that?" he rumbled.

"From Narli, the Crystal Dragon. I freed her from her chains and, in return, she gave me this Serpent Stone. She said that if I gave it to you, you would give me some water from your well." She was shaking from head to toe as she stared up nervously at the hovering creature.

The serpent peered down at her thoughtfully. "You freed the dragon from her bonds?"

Indigo nodded her head mutely.

"Narli is my friend," said the serpent.

"Mine, too," Indigo said in a small voice. "Please, I'll give you this nice shiny Stone if you'll just give me a little water in return," she pleaded, holding up the Stone.

"It's a fair deal," said Ion, hoping to cement the bargain.

The serpent turned his attention to the boy. "Who is this?" he demanded.

Ion stepped protectively in front of Indigo. "I am Prince Ion of Beringer and this is Princess Indigo of Abaddon. We mean you no harm. We only want a little water in exchange for the Serpent Stone," he told him. While he sounded brave, he was trembling inside. This giant creature could easily swallow them both whole with one gulp.

"Just a little water is all we need..." repeated Indigo. "Please?"

"Why should I give you any water?" asked the serpent haughtily.

"I need it to remove my curse," Indigo told him.

"What curse?" inquired the serpent.

Indigo removed one of her silver gauntlets and showed him her discolored hand. "I kill things," she said simply.

The serpent hissed again and retracted its head away from her. "You are a witch?"

"No, it's just a curse. I'm hoping that your water will cure me. We've come a very long way." She slipped her gauntlet back on.

The serpent eyed the Stone. "Hmm…a Serpent Stone…possibly equivalent exchange."

Indigo held the Stone higher, hoping to entice the pondering reptile.

In a flash, the serpent bent forward and snatched the Stone from her hands.

Shocked, Indigo and Ion watched as the creature licked the Stone and then popped it down its throat like a dinner mint. "Umm. . .tasty. . . but not filling."

As they watched in horror, the serpent suddenly rose up to its full height above them. Having lost their bargaining tool, both were certain that they were about to be swallowed up into the belly of the beast. They clutched each other close, prepared for the end.

"Sorry about this," Ion muttered to her. "Me, too," whispered Indigo. Ever loyal, Nyx hunkered down at his mistress's feet and put his paws over his eyes.

As the serpent descended rapidly towards them, they clung to each other desperately and squeezed their eyes shut, bracing for impact. Instead, the serpent whizzed right past them, descending all the way back down into the well. Their eyes popped open and they looked at each other in stunned surprise.

"He's gone!" gasped Indigo.

"Run for it!" shouted Ion, grabbing her hand.

They had gotten only ten feet away when they felt the earth rumbling again. Whirling around, they watched in terror as the monstrous serpent rose up again from the well. This time he held a small bucket in his mouth.

Due to the bucket, he addressed them in a slightly garbled voice. *"Take this waber and go quibly before I change my mind. If I see you again, I will swabble you bof whole!"*

He lowered his head and delivered the bucket into Indigo's hands.

"Th—thank you!" she stammered as she grasped the bucket by its handle. The water sloshed inside.

"Nice doing business," said Ion cordially. "We'll be going now. " He grabbed her arm and they began to slowly back away.

The serpent lowered his head toward them once more and sniffed curiously. "Too bad," he rumbled. "I missed lunch."

Panicked, they turned and ran for their lives. However, they had to slow their pace a bit as the running caused some of the precious water to be lost over the side of the bucket.

Chapter Nine

Concocting the Cure

Led by Bijou, the travelers hastily retreated from the Sacred Well and the Valley of Vervain. They raced back across the level grassland to the base of the rugged hill they had earlier descended. Indigo stood, gazing up the rocky slope in dismay. "That looks even steeper going up."

"Come on, I'll help you," Ion said, grabbing hold of her hand. She raised her other hand, indicating the precious bucket of water. "Okay, but I need to be *very* careful," she cautioned him.

"Do you want me to carry the bucket?" he asked.

"No, I'll carry it. I just have to be very, very careful not to fall—and I hope we don't meet any more burgos," she shuddered at the thought. "I can't afford to be startled again, or I might spill the water."

"The burrows are worse than the burgos, so do mind where you're stepping," Ion cautioned her.

Indigo nodded and carefully started up the hill, clutching the bucket of Sacred Water in one hand and Ion's hand in the other. Step by careful step, they slowly ascended the hill. Indigo made sure each step was securely placed before taking another.   Ion would like to have gone much faster, but he patiently maintained her slow, painstaking pace.

Nyx, however, could not restrain his energy and bounded up and down the hillside several times before the two humans were even half way up.

They were almost at the top of the hill when another disgusting burgo did in fact leap out of a hole about two feet in front of them. Indigo gasped but forced herself to freeze in place.

"Easy does it," Ion encouraged her. He too stopped dead in his tracks, and they both stared at the hairy creature, which brazenly returned their stare. When they did not move or threaten him, the creature was emboldened to approach them.

"He's coming closer," whispered Indigo.

"Boo, shoo,"   Ion tried to wave off the curious burgo.

Ignoring him, the creature continued toward them until he came within sniffing distance of the bucket.

"I think he wants the water," Indigo said panicked. Quickly, she transferred the bucket to her other hand, further away from the creature's snout.

Ion picked up a rock and threw it at the relentless rodent. The burgo dodged the rock but bared its fangs and hissed angrily at them.

"I thought you said they were harmless," cried Indigo in alarm.

"I said *usually*," Ion reminded her. He drew the dagger from his boot and advanced toward the hissing rodent.

"Be careful," warned Indigo. "I don't have a potion for burgo bites."

Just as Ion was about to pounce on the ornery beast, Nyx came dashing down the hill and grabbed the burgo in its teeth, shaking it hard.

"Watch out for his fangs!" Indigo screamed at the wolf.

Nyx tossed the shaken beastie far down the hill where it got unsteadily to its feet and wobbled off away from them.

Indigo patted the wolf approvingly on his silvery head. "Good boy, Nyx. You saved us—and the water." The wolf smiled smugly at Ion, reminding him that he was Indigo's guardian.

Ion snorted. "I was just about to stab it when your wolf ran up and snatched it away."

"Ooh," Indigo frowned at him in dismay. "I didn't want you to kill the poor thing."

"The *poor thing* was about to attack you and steal your water."

"Well, fortunately, Nyx took care of it. The wolf nodded proudly, as if agreeing.

When they finally reached the crest of the hill, they stopped to catch their breath and stood gazing down into the valley below them. It was sunset now and the sky was streaked with wide swaths of rose, orange, and purple. It looked deceptively calm and peaceful.

"We made it!" panted Indigo. "Let's rest a minute." She sat down, planting the bucket securely beside her.

"All right, but only for a few minutes," said Ion as he dropped down beside her. "We need to make camp before sundown."

Nyx hunkered down on his haunches, insinuating himself between his mistress and the boy. Even Bijou came in for a landing and perched on the edge of the hill. He scanned the valley below with his radar making sure that they were not being followed. Fortunately, he detected nothing suspicious.

"Too bad Narli isn't here to give us a lift back," said Indigo.

"No way! I am *not* riding on any more dragons!" Ion said vehemently.

"I thought it was fun," said Indigo.

"That's because you didn't have a wolf clinging to your back the entire trip," he told her, glaring at Nyx.

The wolf narrowed his eyes at him and snorted disapprovingly.

"That serpent certainly wasn't very friendly, was he?" she asked.

"Humph," said Ion. "I think he was too hungry to be friendly."

Overhearing the remark, Bijou squeaked and nodded his head.

"Bijou here almost became his lunch—or at least a small snack," Ion commiserated with the bat.

Bijou nodded urgently and wrapped his wings over his face, not wanting to remember the traumatic incident.

"Poor Bijou," Indigo sympathized with the bat, "You were very brave to look into the well. It must have been perfectly dreadful being swallowed up like that. "

Bijou nodded again and rolled his eyes dramatically to underscore the enormity of his ordeal.

"Well, at least I got my water," said Indigo, tapping the water bucket beside her on the grass. "Now I can mix up my cure."

" I just hope it was worth it," Ion told her. "It was a lot of trouble for a little bucket of water."

"Do you regret coming with me?" she asked him. "I wouldn't blame you if you do. After all, you've been chased by man-eating goats, almost carried off by a harpy, nearly squeezed to death by a killer sunflower, and almost swallowed by a giant serpent. It's a lot to ask of anyone."

"Well, I certainly wouldn't do it for just *anyone*. But for you…I would do it all again," he smiled warmly at her, getting lost in those intense purple blue eyes of hers.

"After everything?" she asked.

He nodded at her, moving closer to her. *"After everything*," he confirmed. She looked particularly gorgeous in the rosy glow of sunset and her full lips looked awfully inviting…   Between them, Nyx suddenly stood up and shook himself, ruining the moment.

Ion glared in annoyance at the intervening wolf but then reluctantly leapt to his feet as well. "Nyx is right. We need to keep moving while we still have some light. He extended a hand to Indigo, pulling her up.   He turned to the bat, " Bijou, find us a good campsite."

Bijou flew ahead of them into the woods. They followed him through the dense forest until they came to an open area that was protected on all sides by tall trees. A small stream trickled nearby.   The bat squeaked, nodding at Ion to indicate his choice of campsite.

"Okay," said Ion, surveying the area.   "This looks like a good spot. We've even got water nearby so we can wash up. If I were you, Bijou, I'd rinse off that slimy serpent saliva."   He sniffed in the direction of the hovering bat.   "No offense, but you're starting to smell a bit ripe."

Bijou sniffed under his wing and made a face. Immediately, he dived into the stream and splashed about vigorously to cleanse himself.   Nyx jumped in after the bat, causing a wall of water to unexpectedly drench Bijou. Coughing, the bat retaliated by dive-bombing the wolf, hydroplaning water into the wolf's face.   The unlikely pair continued to frolic in the water, evidently enjoying each other's company.

"I think Nyx has made a new friend," laughed Indigo, observing the two in the water.

"Looks like they have the right idea," said Ion as he sniffed under his own arm. "Think I'd better join them." He lifted his shirt off over his head, tossed it to the ground, and leapt into the water along with Nyx and Bijou.

Indigo stood a moment, observing the trio splashing happily in the water. She watched as Ion picked up a stick and threw it downstream. The wolf immediately bounded off and retrieved it. She smiled to herself. Looks like Nyx has made another new friend, she thought. It was highly unusual for the wolf to bond with anyone other than herself. He was even a bit guarded with her father. She felt a pang of conscience as she thought of her father. She hoped he wasn't worrying too much about her. She regretted now that in her haste to leave she had neglected to leave a note for him. Oh well, she would be back soon and then she would explain everything to him.

Indigo laughed as the cavorting trio splashed her with water. "Come in," urged Ion. "The water's wonderful."

Removing her boots, she lifted her dress a modest few inches and waded in to join them. The water felt cool and refreshing around her ankles. "That does feel heavenly," she said. "I wish I could take a proper bath."

Ion noted that she had lovely feet and ankles. "I could turn my back if you'd like to go for a dip," he offered. "I promise I won't look."

"Maybe tomorrow," she said, "if all goes well."

"If what goes well?" he asked.

"My cure. I'm anxious to get started on it," she told him.

He glanced at her in surprise. "You're going to do it here, tonight?"

"Why not?" she asked him. "I have everything I need now to make it…and I've waited long enough."

"I guess," said Ion, shrugging. "If you're sure you're ready."

"Oh, I'm ready!" she exclaimed. "I've been ready my whole life."

Behind them, Nyx barked excitedly as he jumped about in the stream. They turned to see that he was holding a large flapping fish in his mouth.

"*Thatta boy*, Nyx!" Ion shouted. "I could use a fish dinner."

However, as they watched, the fish flipped its way free and slipped back into the water.

Hooting in disappointment, Ion and Nyx both dove after the disappearing fish. Seconds later, Ion reemerged from the water with the fish in his hands and held it triumphantly over his head. "Got it!"

He must have jinxed himself because the vigorous fish succeeded in wriggling away once again and splashed back into the water. Again, Nyx and Ion dove into the water in pursuit of the elusive fish.

Indigo cheered on the pair. She wouldn't mind a fish dinner herself.

Suddenly, the wily fish broke the surface near Indigo and leapt high into the air. Both Nyx and Ion leapt up to grab it—and so did Indigo. In their haste, the three of them collided in the air. Indigo fell forward with a splash and landed on the stream bank smack on top of Ion. Because her hands were raised over her head, her face came to rest on his. They were nose to nose—and lips to lips. Did he just kiss her? Or was he just moving his head, causing their lips to brush accidentally? They stared into each other's eyes for a long, stunned moment then she quickly rolled off of him.

Sitting up, she was somewhat surprised to see that the fish was wedged firmly between her clasped gauntlets. *"Dinner,"* she said, waving the fish.

Indigo had just piled up a large mound of dry twigs and brush for the fire when Ion rejoined her. His wet hair was slicked back and he had changed into a fresh white shirt emblazoned with the letter *'B'* (for Beringer). She glanced at him approvingly as he knelt next to her. She could smell his clean, masculine scent. As he had in the cave, he started a fire by striking his dagger against the flint.

"You look nice," she said glad that he couldn't see her blushing in the dusky light.

"Thanks," he told her as he blew on the embers. "I always try to dress for dinner. But this is my last shirt, so I hope it survives the journey home." The fire quickly took hold and Ion slipped the fish onto a makeshift spit fashioned from a branch and laid it over the flames.

"Dinner will be ready shortly, madam," he informed her.

"Good. I'm famished!" she exclaimed. Running for your life seemed to work up quite an appetite.

"Me, too!" he agreed. "I could eat a stuffed water buffalo. But I'll settle for a nice fat fish."

They sat companionably beside each other at the fire, watching as the fish cooked, crackling and popping appetizingly, over the flames. Nyx hunkered down on the other side of Indigo, eagerly sniffing the aromatic fish, while Bijou perched nearby, enjoying the warmth of the fire.

When he judged that the fish was done, Ion slipped it off the spit and divvied it up between them, including Nyx. Bijou was already busy dining on a menu of local fireflies.

They made short work of the delectable fish. "You're an excellent cook," Indigo praised him. Ordinarily, she wasn't too fond of fish, but hunger definitely broadened one's tastes.

"It's good we'll have full bellies to begin our journey home tomorrow," said Ion.

Indigo looked askance at him. "Do we have to return the same way we came?" she asked. "I'd rather not have to go back through the Enchanted Forest and the Haunted Forest. What if we meet those goats again?" she asked, shuddering. "Not to mention the harpies and killer sunflowers."

Ion turned to the bat. "What do you think, Bijou? Can you find us another way home?"

The bat thought for a long moment but then shook his head glumly. If there had been an easier way, he would have taken it on the outbound journey. There was only one way there and one way back. And unfortunately he couldn't promise that the return trip would be any easier.

"Oh well," said Ion. "At least we know what to watch out for this time."

"Yeah...everything," Indigo muttered.

"Listen," he said. "You might want to hold off on that cure until we get back..."

"Why?" she asked sharply.

He shrugged. "Well, you did kill a monster harpy and a giant sunflower that was about to eat me...I'm just saying..." he trailed off, hoping she wouldn't take offense.

"You think I should keep the curse so I can kill more things?" she asked, looking outraged.

"No! Well...maybe just the ones that are trying to eat us..." he added lamely.

She leapt to her feet and began pacing in front of the fire.

He jumped up too, wishing he hadn't brought up the obviously touchy topic. Now he feared she was mad at him.

"I don't want to kill anything else!" she exclaimed. "Not even if it's chasing us. I'd rather take my chances than remain a monster."

"Sorry," he apologized. "I didn't mean to upset you."

"I know," she told him. "You just don't know what it's been like to have to live with this." She raised her gauntlets. "It's always been a part of me. And every day of my life I've hated it! It's all I can think of. Do you understand? It's impossible to think of anything—or anyone else! The sooner I'm cured, the sooner I can get on with my life."

"I get it," he said, nodding his head in sympathy. "If I were cursed, I'd probably feel the same as you. Let me know if I can help," he told her, looking chastened.

"Thank you," she said. "I'm glad you understand that this can't wait even another minute."

Opening her bag, she drew out a cloth and spread it out in front of the fire. Ion and Nyx looked on expectantly and both crept forward onto the cloth. Indigo glanced up at them. "If you don't mind, it's better if you stay back. That means you, too, Nyx." Grumbling, the wolf edged backwards off the edge of the cloth, as did Ion.

One by one, Indigo pulled out various bottles and potions and arranged them on the cloth in front of her. Lastly, she took out the ancient volume and opened it to the bookmarked page, *A Cure All for Curses*. She scanned the listed ingredients carefully to make sure she had not overlooked anything. One by one, she added all of the required items into a small bottle, including the vial of Life Everlasting, which Zozimo had given her.

"All right. I think that's everything I need but the water." She glanced up at him. "Ion, would you please hand me the bucket?"

Ion jumped to his feet and started toward the bucket, which lay about ten feet away. Suddenly, he tripped and fell face forward over a hidden rock, landing not too far away from the bucket.

"Be careful!" warned Indigo. "If you spill that water, I'll be cursed forever!"

117

"Not too much pressure," Ion said, getting carefully to his feet. With exaggerated caution, he picked up the bucket, walked back very slowly, and handed it to her.

"May I please borrow your dagger?" she asked him.

"Sure," he said, surprised at the request. He pulled the dagger from his boot and gave it to her.

Ion watched as she tilted the bucket so that all the water ran to one side. Clutching the dagger, she stabbed the bucket on the other side, creating a small hole. Very carefully, she allowed the water to drip through the hole into the small bottle, which held the prepared potion. Then she corked the bottle and shook it vigorously.

"It will take a few minutes for the molecules to interact with each other." She looked at Ion and Nyx. 'You might want to move back." They both scuttled back a few inches.

In amazement, they all watched as the bottle began to glow brightly. "Wow!" exclaimed Ion. "Maybe this will work after all."

She held up the glowing bottle to the firelight. "Just think, in a few minutes I could be cured!"

Ion nodded at her eagerly. "Go ahead. Try it!" For her sake, he prayed it would work.

With some trepidation, Indigo lifted the bubbling beaker. She was just about to uncork the bottle when she saw Ion's eyes roll up before he passed out beside her!

"Ion?!" she shouted in alarm.

Nyx barked furiously but he too suddenly went silent and fell over.

"What's happening?" Indigo cried in confusion. Before she could find out, she was also overcome and fainted dead away beside Ion and Nyx.

Dash swept into view, chuckling as he continued to sprinkle his fairy dust on the slumbering trio. "Nightie night!" smirked the fairy. Carefully, he took the still stoppered bottle from Indigo's gauntlet. "Zimbardo is going to love this!"

Tucking the potion safely away in his robe, Dash hoisted Indigo over his shoulder and flew off. (Fortunately, as noted before, fairy dust makes everyone quite light. In fact, it was much in demand throughout the Five Kingdoms as a reputed weight loss miracle drug.)

Bijou had been sleeping upside-down in a nearby tree. Belatedly, he spied the fairy but was too late to stop Indigo's abduction. Shaking his head in distress, the bat flapped away urgently, chasing after Indigo as she was carried off into the night by the fairy henchman.

Chapter Ten

Zimbardo Strikes Back

When Indigo opened her eyes, she was laying on the ground. It was so completely dark that for a moment she feared she was blind. She blinked repeatedly until her eyes adjusted to the darkness. "Hello?" she whispered into the gloom. "Is anyone there?" But there was no answer. Tentatively, she stirred her limbs and was shocked to realize that both her hands and feet were chained. Where was she and how had she gotten there? And what had become of Ion and Nyx? She rolled her head from side to side but could make out little in the heavy darkness.

She felt panic flooding through her but forced herself to remain calm and make no sound. Quietly, she wriggled until she managed to sit upright She struggled against the chains binding her hands and feet, but succeeded only in bruising her wrists and ankles. As she was not chained to anything, she might possibly lie down again and try rolling, but where could she go? The air around her was still and stale, so she reasoned that she must be captive inside a room somewhere—or more likely, she feared, a dungeon. She froze as she heard heavy footsteps approaching. A door creaked open and a dark silhouette filled the doorframe.

"Welcome to my humble abode, Princess Indigo," a deep, eerie voice rumbled in the darkness.

"Who…who are you?" she asked tremulously.

The dark figure stepped into the room and with a wave of his hand, ignited the torches that hung on the surrounding walls. "I am Zimbardo, the great and powerful!" he announced in lordly tones. With a nod of his head, he caused her to rise up into the air.

"Put me down!" she shrieked in midair.

Gently, he caused her to float into a plush, high-backed chair. Her heart was hammering in her chest as she gazed up at the imposing, dark-robed figure who loomed over her. "Wizard?" she whispered.

"Sorcerer!" he corrected her. "We're much prettier than wizards." He preened his hair and swirled his cape vainly as he strutted in front of her. "Don't you think?" he turned to her expectantly. He was dressed all in black, except for the crimson velvet lining of his cape. She noted the striking crystal amulet, which hung from his neck. She shuddered, thinking he looked more like a vampire.

"Why am I here?" she managed to ask as her wits began to return.

"You've got no idea, have you?" he asked as he crossed the room towards her. "I'm surprised that your father never told you about me."

Now that he was standing directly in front of her, she could see that he was older than she had first thought. Though still undeniably handsome, Zimbardo's face was showing its middle age—despite his assiduous application of the best anti-aging potions. There were lines around his eyes and mouth and grey at his temples, though the rest of his hair was suspiciously jet black and swept back into a high pompadour. Though he appeared vain to the point of foppishness, Indigo sensed it would be a great mistake to underestimate his potential menace.

"How do you know my father?" she asked in a stronger voice. There was something about this ominous man that seemed almost familiar in a vague sort of way. Who was he?

"Oh, your father and I go *way* back. I knew your mother too…" He stared meaningfully into her eyes. "She was very beautiful…such a shame what happened to her." He smiled mockingly.

Indigo gasped and her hair stood on end as she suddenly realized exactly who he was. "It was *you,* wasn't it?" she cried. "You're the one responsible for this terrible curse."

Zimbardo nodded, "I confess it was I." He leered at her from head to foot. "You're as beautiful as your mother."

Indigo struggled to her feet. "Let me go, you monster!"

"Sit down!" With another nod of his head, he caused her to slam back heavily into the chair. "You are my *guest*...indefinitely." He approached her, peering closely into her face. "So, it's true," he said. "Your eyes *are* the color of indigo, most unusual and beguiling." He lowered his face to hers as if to kiss her.

Alarmed, she spat in his face, glaring at him with ice-cold eyes.

He flashed her a murderous look, sending a chill down her spine. However, he quickly recovered himself. Calmly, he withdrew a handkerchief from his vest pocket and wiped the spittle from his face.

"I'm actually quite charming once you get to know me." He smiled smugly.

"Why did you do it?" she asked. Clearly, he was not going to release her, so she might as well get the answers to some long held questions.

Zimbardo heaved a melodramatic sigh. "Oh, it's the usual long, sad story, I fear. I was in love with your mother, and she was in love with me...until your back-stabbing father stole her away from me."

"I don't believe you," she cried.

"I assure you it's true. Citrine betrayed me and broke my heart." He sighed again. "She cost me many a sleepless night."

"If you loved her, why did you curse her and let her die?" she asked.

"I didn't kill your mother. She died giving birth to you. I had nothing to do with her death. I mourned her terribly. I still do." Such a look of sadness washed over his face, that Indigo thought she actually believed him. For a moment, she pitied him.

"But why did you curse me? she pressed.

"Your parents had to be punished for taking what was rightfully mine. Tragically, I lost my queen that day...as well as my kingdom." He bent low, leering into her face. "But now I have you. *"*

"Me?" she asked in horrified disbelief. "What do you want with me?"

"I couldn't have your mother, but now I shall have you." He flashed her what he considered his most charming smile, though it only sent a shudder of repulsion through her body.

"Never!" Indigo cried. "I will never consent to it! You must be mad!"

He reached out, grasping her chained hands. She tried to pull them away, but he held them firmly. One by one, he lifted them to his lips, kissing the back of each silver gauntlet. "I am mad...mad for you."

She pulled away her hands, suppressing another shudder. "Keep away from me!"

"I don't mean to frighten you. I know this must all seem a bit sudden. After all, you've only just met me, and here I am pouring out my heart like a poor, lovesick fool. You must forgive me if I'm over eager; it 's just that I've waited so long."

He gestured to the wall behind Indigo, which displayed portraits of her from infancy to the present day. "I have watched you grow up from a darling baby into an exquisite young woman."

Indigo twisted around in her chair. She was not after all, in a dungeon but rather Zimbardo's dank and dusty library. She stared incredulously at the numerous portraits of herself lining the walls. "You've been watching me all this time?" she said aghast.

He nodded at her. "I'm a very patient man, Princess. I have waited a long time for you to come of age. Now you will keep the promise that your mother broke and marry me."

"I'd rather die!" Indigo shouted at him. The idea of marrying him was beyond repellant. She'd rather remain a spinster forever—or die young.

"Oh, come now. I'm not *that* bad. Sure, there's an age difference, but I'm still rather dashing, don't you think?" He admired himself in a large mirror nearby. (Though undiagnosed in his time, Zimbardo was clearly a raging narcissist as well as a deviant psychopath.)

Looking ill, Indigo shook her head, stifling a gag.

Zimbardo appeared a bit crestfallen. "Oh well...physical attraction isn't everything. What if I can still make marriage worth your while?"

"What do you mean?" she asked warily.

He reached into his vest pocket and pulled out the bottle with the stolen cure. "Marry me and I will remove your curse." He waved the bottle in front of her face.

"That's mine!" Indigo exclaimed in shock. "You stole it from me!" She tried to snatch away the bottle, but he pulled it away easily, holding it over her head.

"You want the cure?" he asked, clearly toying with her.

She nodded urgently. "I went to a lot of trouble to get that cure. You have no idea what I've been through."

"Oh, but I *do* know…everything…" he gloated. "Who do you think sent you that helpful book?"

Realization washed over her, causing her to feel sick. "You're my Secret Admirer?"

"Surprise!" he smirked.

Indigo wrinkled her nose in disgust. "Is the cure even real or is it just another one of your tricks?"

"Oh, it's very real. Trust me, I would not have risked your life if it weren't necessary to obtain the cure. Sorry about the serpent."

"Really?" she asked, not quite buying it. "Can't you just wave your hand or something and undo the curse?"

"Actually, it's not that simple. I'm afraid my black magic is far too potent to be easily undone even by me. But don't worry. Once we're married, I will return the cure to you."

"And if I refuse?" she asked boldly.

He shook his head sadly. "That would be a shame as I would have to kill everyone you care about. I know you love your father, so I have allowed him to live…until now… The choice is yours: marry me and be cured or refuse me and be the cause of your father's painful death."

Indigo sighed heavily. She had no doubt that he would follow through on his coldblooded threat if she refused him. "All right…just leave my father alone."

"Excellent!" he cried jubilantly. "I'll take that as a *yes*."

Indigo bowed her head and buried her face in her hands. Her life was over, but it would be a worthwhile sacrifice if she could save her father.

"Don't look so glum, my beloved," cooed the hovering sorcerer. "You've made the right choice." In fact, I think it's time we shared our happy news with your father. Hopefully, he'll give us his blessing. Now, if you'll excuse me, I have some…preparations…to make for the happy event." He turned on his booted heel and started toward the door.

"Wait!" cried Indigo. He paused expectantly. "I was traveling with Prince Ion and my wolf, Nyx. Do you know what became of them?"

He shrugged, shaking his head with feigned innocence. "I have no idea...but I wouldn't count on seeing either of them any time soon." He turned and exited the library.

Dash had his ear to the library door and only narrowly avoided being knocked over as Zimbardo exited abruptly.

"Congratulate me, I'm engaged!" smirked the sorcerer.

"You're not going to give her the cure, are you?" said Dash.

The sorcerer laughed and shrugged ambivalently. "I think she's perfect the way she is. Finish the preparations. We leave tomorrow night."

"Must I do everything?" whined the fairy. "Aren't you going to help me?"

Zimbardo glared at Dash and rubbed his thumb over the crystal amulet, causing an electric shock to jolt through the fairy. "If you can't handle the job, you whining little flea, I can replace you."

"S...sorry, Master," shook the fairy miserably. "Could I at least have a dinner break?"

The sorcerer glared at him darkly, once more poising his thumb over the amulet.

"Cancel that. I'm not hungry." Before the sorcerer could zap him again, the fairy turned and flitted off to finish the preparations.

Zimbardo shook his head. *"Fairies!"* he muttered. Disgusted, he turned and stalked off down the long, torch-lit hallway.

* * *

Hovering outside the library window, Bijou had observed all and was filled with a terrible dread. The princess could not have fallen into worse hands. Zimbardo was known to be the most evil sorcerer in the Five Kingdoms. If she were to be saved, he must get help at once. He flew off into the night literally *like a bat out of hell.*

As he flew nonstop, Bijou reached the campsite within the hour. He found Ion and Nyx still passed out beside the now low burning fire. After his most high-pitched squeal failed to wake them, he tried slapping them in the face with his wings.

Ion raised an arm and *batted* him away like an annoying mosquito but did not wake.   Exasperated, the bat grabbed up the discarded bucket from the Sacred Well. Holding it in his mouth, he dipped it into the stream. Despite the small hole in the side made by the dagger, it still held a good amount of water.   Flying back, he doused the sleeping pair with the water, finally succeeding in rousing them.

Sputtering, Ion sat up, rubbing the water from his eyes. For a moment, he was completely disoriented.   One moment he had been sitting next to Indigo at the fire, helping her mix up her cure, and the next moment all had gone black—*Indigo!* What had happened to her? He jumped to his feet and searched the campsite.   She was nowhere to be found.

Beside him, Nyx also scrambled to his feet. He sniffed about desperately trying to pick up Indigo's scent, but shook his head at Ion.

Finally, Ion noticed the bat, which was hovering above them, madly trying to get their attention. "Bijou, did you see what happened?"

The bat nodded frantically.

"Do you know where Indigo is?" Again the bat nodded urgently, pointing off into the distance.

"She went for a walk?" he guessed.

The bat frowned at him, shaking his head.

"Did someone take her?" he asked.

Bijou nodded affirmatively, continuing to point urgently into the distance.

"Who was it?" he demanded, as if the bat could tell him.

Frustrated, Bijou tried to mime sprinkling them with fairy dust. To illustrate, he picked up some dirt and sprinkled it over Ion's head.

"Hey, knock it off," he said, brushing the soil from his hair. "Someone put dirt in her hair?" he guessed lamely.

Desperate, the bat drew a finger under his throat, trying to underscore the extremity of her peril.

"She's in trouble?" he deduced at last.

Finally, he got it! The wingless ones could be so slow at times.

The bat nodded at him and flew off ahead, urgently motioning for him to follow.

Ion turned to the wolf. " We've got to help Indigo!"

Barking his agreement, the wolf turned tail and raced off after the bat.

"Hey, wait for me!" shouted Ion. He was fast but no match for the fleet-footed wolf.   Glancing behind him, the wolf snorted in disgust at the boy's relative slowness.   As there was no time to lose, he ran back to the boy and abruptly scooped him up onto his back.

"Oh…all right!" Ion gasped in surprise as he found himself balancing awkwardly atop the wolf's back.   He had often seen Indigo ride on the wolf's back, but he was a good deal taller.   Tucking up his long legs like a jockey, he flattened himself out on the wolf's back and threw his arms around his neck, hanging on for dear life.   Nyx tore off into the night, following after Bijou.

They ran all night, making only one stop when Ion accidentally fell asleep and rolled off the wolf's back. Though everyone was bone-tired, they continued on doggedly, running back through the Enchanted Forest and then the Haunted Forest. They were running so fast during the wee hours of the morning that the bizarre inhabitants did little more than blink at them as they dashed past.

It was mid-morning when they finally arrived back at Zozimo's Shop. Bijou got there first and could see the wizard dozing in his chair by the fire. He flew in through the open window and landed on the arm of his chair, startling him awake.

"Bijou! What is it?" he rasped in alarm.

The bat leaned over, appearing to whisper in the wizard's ear.

Disturbed by the news, Zozimo was now on his feet, pacing in front of the fire. "Zimbardo has her? I knew he was up to something. That's why I've been jamming his channels."

Bijou nodded his head vigorously.

"You say he plans to marry her?" the wizard squinted at him, deep in thought.

The bat nodded again.

"I can't allow it!" exclaimed the wizard.

Bijou shook his head vehemently.

"We'll have to stop him!" exclaimed the wizard with certainty.

Bijou nodded, waiting expectantly.

The wizard ruminated. "We need a plan…"

Bijou nodded, waving his wings impatiently. Sometimes even the wizard could be a bit slow.

"I'm thinking," he chided the bat. "Where's Ion?"

At that moment, Nyx leapt in through the open window with the boy still clinging to his back.

Ion rolled unceremoniously off the wolf's back and staggered to his feet. Urgently, he confronted Zozimo. "Indigo's gone! We have to find her!"

Panting heavily beside him, Nyx fiercely nodded his agreement at the wizard.

"Yes, yes, I know…she's been abducted by the sorcerer, Zimbardo."

Ion was taken aback. "How do you know that?"

"A little bat told me," said the wizard.

Bijou waved a wing at Ion.

Ion glared at Zozimo. "You knew, didn't you? You knew she was the princess the whole time, and you didn't tell me," he accused him.

Zozimo shrugged. "Who do you think made her those fine silver gauntlets?"

"Why didn't you tell me who she was?" demanded Ion.

The wizard shrugged again. "I thought it was better if you didn't know. You might have been scared off if I told you she was really *Princess Death*, I believe you called her?"

Ion shrugged in embarrassment. "That was before I got to know her. You still should have told me."

"Nevermind that now. We can do formal introductions later. Zimbardo is holding the princess captive at his castle. Apparently, he's planning a wedding."

"A wedding? Who's getting married?" Ion asked in surprise.

"Guess…" said the wizard ruefully.

Ion gasped in horror. "Oh no! We've got to stop it! Let's go!" Immediately, he turned and started toward the door followed by Nyx.

But Zozimo pulled him back with his long staff. "Wait!" he ordered.

"What are you doing? We have to go!" Ion sputtered indignantly, tumbling back into the room.

"We need a plan," said the wizard.

"I have a plan!" shouted Ion impatiently. "I'm going to go to Zimbardo's castle and rescue Indigo!"

"It may be too late," warned the wizard. "He's planning to take her back to Abaddon for the ceremony."

"Then we'll go to Abaddon. Come on!" Again, he turned and started toward the door.

This time Zozimo knocked him on the head with his staff. "Hold your horses, lad!"

"Oww! Why did you hit me?" he asked, rubbing his head.

"Think before you act!" the wizard scolded him. "We need to gather some important elements first. After all, Zimbardo is no ordinary sorcerer. We'll have to fight magic with magic."

Chapter Eleven

A Good Day for a Black Wedding

A large black cloud floated ominously over the full moon, casting a long rolling shadow over the countryside below. Concealed inside the black cloud was a very ornate black carriage drawn by a single magnificent black steed. Clad in a long black coat and top hat, Dash was perched precariously atop the driver's seat, steering the carriage high into the night sky.

Inside the carriage, the captive princess was forced to sit uncomfortably close beside Zimbardo. Her hands and feet were still chained, but she did her best to inch away from the odious sorcerer, so that her body would not accidentally brush his. Turning away from him, she peered out of the carriage window, marveling as they flew through the night.

Deliberately, Zimbardo leaned closely over her shoulder. "Enjoying the ride?"

She averted her head in disgust, squirming away from him as far as possible.

"Just think, soon you'll be Mrs. Zimbardo." He leered at her with lewd anticipation.

Inwardly, Indigo groaned. *"Mrs. Zimbardo*? Really?! How low could a girl go? She wanted to scream and thrash him, but she forced herself to remain calm. She knew she must keep her wits about her if there was any hope of escaping the vengeful sorcerer.

"A powerful man like you could have anyone, I'm sure," she flattered him. "What do you want with me? I'm just an awkward, silly girl with no experience of the world. Certainly, you could find a wife more accomplished than me," she hinted.

"More polished, perhaps," he nodded. "But you have something very special that is beyond all value."

"What are you talking about?" she asked, sincerely puzzled.

"You alone have *the touch of death,* a gift which I bestowed upon you," he confided proudly.

"Gift?!" she exclaimed. "Your gift has ruined my entire life!"

"From now on, you will see it quite differently," he promised. "With you by my side, we'll be the ultimate power couple. Just think of it—my potent black magic combined with your lethal touch—why, we'll be unstoppable."

Indigo's eyes widened in horror as she realized his true intent and the depth of his twisted depravity. She had not seen that coming. He was planning to *exploit* her curse, not remove it! "You can force me to marry you, but you can't force me to kill for you," she glared at him.

"I like your feisty spirit, Princess. Don't worry, in time you'll see it's fun to have power over others. Besides, you forget that I'm only letting your father live as long as you are…cooperative.*"* He smiled at her darkly.

"If I agree to your demands, will you return the cure to me?"

He shrugged indifferently, "After you help me conquer the Five Kingdoms…we'll see…"

Indigo lapsed into brooding silence. She feared he really was mad and beyond all reasoning.

* * *

Back in Abaddon, King Azrael had been beside himself with worry and remorse since Indigo's departure. He blamed himself bitterly for the unfortunate demise of Lord Lurch and would never forgive himself if something were to happen to his beloved daughter. He had tried desperately to find her, sending out his troops repeatedly, but to no avail.

On this night he sat deep in gloom upon his throne, attempting to attend to the legal business of the court, though his heart was not in it. The throne room was crowded with royal officials and attendants, as well as the common people waiting to make their appeals to the court.

The king lifted his head hopefully as a guardsman entered the chamber and strode rapidly towards him. "Have you news of the princess?" he asked eagerly.

The guardsman knelt humbly before him. "I'm sorry, Your Highness, we've searched the Five Kingdoms but there's still no report of Princess Indigo."

"Then keep searching! I must find her!" the king cried despondently.

A thunderous rapping at the chamber door startled the entire court. "Who's that knocking at my door?" cried the king.

The king's guards raced toward the door but before they could reach it, it burst open.

In a shocking entrance, Zimbardo stormed into the throne room, clutching Princess Indigo to his side. As her hands and feet remained chained, she could do little more than shuffle forward. A hovering Dash held onto her other arm in case she attempted to bolt.

The king gasped as he caught sight of his daughter. "Indigo!"

"Father!" she cried, struggling futilely to free herself.

The king rose to his feet to go to his daughter, but Zimbardo nodded at him, causing him to fly back abruptly into his throne.

The king's guardsmen rushed Zimbardo but found themselves suddenly stuck in place, unable to move or speak. Panicked, the rest of the court attempted to flee but were likewise stopped in their tracks.

"A touching family reunion…well…almost," Zimbardo smirked at the king.

"Zimbardo! I should have guessed you were behind this. Release her at once!" demanded the king.

132

"I assure you that I mean your daughter no harm, Azrael. I hold her in the highest esteem. In fact, I plan to wed her."

"No, you can't have her!" the king shouted in horror.

"Oh, yes I can!" Zimbardo shouted back. He muttered a dark incantation and waved his hands.

Immediately, a host of shadowy demons rose up through the floor and filled the room.

The sorcerer clapped his hands. "Prepare my bride!"

Half a dozen fashionably dressed demons stepped forward. They were swathed in a multitude of colors and draped with flamboyant accessories. Their nails were long and sharp and painted in vivid colors with the latest gothic decor.

Indigo struggled as they descended upon her. Paying her no heed, they lifted her effortlessly into the air and whisked her from the throne room.

"Stop!" cried the king. "Where are you taking her?"

Zimbardo turned his attention back to the distraught king. "Don't worry, she's in good hands. You can thank me later for bringing your daughter safely back home," he smiled mockingly.

"I should have killed you a long time ago," the king said grimly.

"I'm just settling an old score. This kingdom would have been mine if you hadn't taken Citrine from me. Now I'll finally be the King of Abaddon, and Indigo will be my queen...once you're removed."

King Azrael struggled to rise from his throne, but Zimbardo nodded at him again, instantly sticking him in place, as he had done with the guards.

The sorcerer crossed over to the motionless king and whispered maliciously in his ear. "The best part about this spell is that even though you can't move, you can still see and hear everything that's happening around you. "

Laughing wickedly, Zimbardo turned and stalked away from the helpless king. "Time to get this party started!" he declared triumphantly.

The demons clapped in agreement and flew off in a dozen different directions.

The Fashion Demons deposited Indigo before the vanity table in her bedchamber. She was shocked to see her devoted maid frozen in place nearby.

"Abigail!" she cried, turning towards her. Unfortunately, her maid could do little more than stare back at her with a distraught expression.

Impatiently, the Fashion Demons twisted her back to face the mirror and began dabbing her face with ghoulish makeup. Indigo stared numbly into the mirror as they rimmed her eyes in black liner and created the ultimate smoky eye, melding brown over purple to accent her eyes. Using large tweezers, two of the demons went to work on her brows. She grimaced in pain, as they seemed to pluck out half of her beautiful thick brows, shaping them into high, thin arches. Next, a deep ruby blush was liberally dusted onto the apples of her cheeks. Lastly, they outlined exaggerated bows over her lips and colored them in with a dark red lipstick. Indigo hardly recognized herself. *Hi there, Mrs. Zimbardo*, she thought, morbidly.

When her makeup was complete, a demon stylist with green cornrows twisted up her long dark hair into a very high topknot and threaded it through with gleaming black pearls. Long tendrils of hair were left along her cheeks and curled into ringlets.

As Indigo watched in amazement, a shimmering black lace wedding gown with a long train floated into the room. The demons twittered excitedly over the beautiful gown. Abruptly, they pulled Indigo to her feet. With her chained hands held over her head, her old lavender gown was quickly ripped off, and the elegant black wedding dress was dropped over her head. It was sleeveless and strapless and fit her like a skin-tight glove. Indigo gasped at her curvaceous reflection. Despite herself, she had to admit it was an exquisite gown. The shimmering black lace reminded her of the starry midnight sky. The Fashion Demons assembled around her, twittering their approval.

Two extravagant, black high-heeled slippers materialized in front of her. They shimmered like her dress and were studded with black diamonds and pearls. The demons lifted Indigo out of her clunky travel boots and into the ethereal slippers. Like the dress, they fit perfectly, as if they had been molded to her feet.

The demons paced around Indigo, critically studying their creation. Strands of lavish black pearls and diamonds accented by gleaming red rubies were wrapped around her neck. But Indigo protested when they tried to remove her mother's beautiful earrings.

"Please, don't harm them. They belonged to my mother."

Shrugging, one of the demons set the sparkling earrings aside on the vanity table. They were replaced with opulent new earrings of the same design as the necklaces. Finally satisfied, the demons spritzed her with a cloud of powder and perfume, causing her to choke.

Back in the throne room, the king and the rest of the court remained motionless in place, unwilling witnesses to Zimbardo's unholy *Black Wedding* preparations. They could only look on in horror as the sorcerer summoned a host of Interior Design Demons. Some clutched blueprints of the room, while others wore tool belts or had measuring tapes draped over their necks.

As the demons clustered around him, Zimbardo gestured dramatically about the room, attempting to convey his vision for the ultimate Goth wedding. Huge chandeliers of silver and sparkling red crystal were swiftly hung from the ceiling. A long black carpet was unspooled from the entrance of the room up to the raised dais of the throne. Unnatural black flowers were everywhere twisted onto gold velvet ropes. In all, the bizarre trappings were really quite splendidly decadent and beautiful.

Satisfied with his wedding decor, Zimbardo turned his attention back to King Azrael. Approaching the motionless king, he lifted the jeweled crown from his head. "You won't be needing this anymore," he gloated. Standing directly in front of Azrael so that the king could see him clearly, he placed the crown upon his own head. "Do I look *kingly?*" he mocked him.

Critically, he regarded the bareheaded king still sitting on his golden throne. "You won't be needing that either." With a wave of his hand, he caused King Azrael to rise up out of the throne and be flung across the room. The king hit the wall with a sickening thud and slid to the ground. Dazed, he sat slumped motionless against the wall.

With great pleasure, Zimbardo approached the vacant throne and sat down with a contented sigh. He wiggled his posterior into the plush seat cushion. "Ah, that feels just right." Distracted, he sat a moment, imagining all the awful things he would do when he was king. Snapping out of his reverie, he rose abruptly to his feet. "But I mustn't keep my bride waiting."

As he stood, his glance fell upon his travel worn black cape and boots. "Oh dear, I can't be married in this shabby attire. I'll need something befitting a king…elegant but not predictable…flashy yet not gaudy…"

More of the artful Fashion Demons clustered around Zimbardo, consulting each other and taking hasty measurements. An ornate black dressing screen materialized behind the throne, and they motioned the sorcerer behind it. Zimbardo disappeared behind the screen followed by the demons. Moments later, he emerged wearing a flamboyant black ensemble studded with flashy gemstones. Under the crown, his black pompadour was slicked back even higher.

Zimbardo peered approvingly at his reflection in the full-length mirror held up by the Fashion Demons. "Now that's more like it." The demons nodded and smiled, giving him a bizarre thumbs up with their painted claws.

* * *

Back in Zozimo's shop, Ion, Bijou, and the wizard were busily preparing for war. The bat was carefully measuring a black powder into small packets to make deadly *potion bombs*. He tucked the finished packets into an artillery belt, which he had slung over his shoulder.

Zozimo and Ion stood over a large crystal cauldron, mixing up the seething contents. Anxious to rescue his mistress, Nyx could do little more than whine and pace nervously about the shop. Curiously, he poked his snout into the roiling cauldron.

"Stay back, Nyx!" warned Ion. "Even a drop of this could kill you."

Grunting in alarm, Nyx jumped back a safe distance behind the crystal cauldron.

The wizard stirred the foaming contents briskly. "All right, all we need now is a phoenix feather. Bijou—"

The bat fetched the feather from the storeroom and returned it to Zozimo, who dropped it into the bubbling potion. Immediately, the potion began to glow and change color. "Now it's ready," pronounced the wizard gravely.

He lifted his staff and dipped the end into the cauldron. When he withdrew the staff, the entire length was glowing.

Ion dipped his dagger into the cauldron, and it too began to glow brightly. "Nice!" said Ion, impressed. "This stuff must really be strong."

"Very…whatever you do, don't touch it," cautioned the wizard.

Ion was dismayed when his dagger suddenly stopped glowing, as did Zozimo's staff. "Hey, what happened?"

"Don't worry. It's even more powerful now," the wizard assured him. "The glowing simply indicates that the reaction has taken place."

"Will it kill Zimbardo?" asked Ion, brandishing his dagger.

"Let's find out," replied the wizard.

Gathering up their weapons, they rushed out of the shop followed eagerly by Nyx and Bijou.

Once outside, Ion suddenly pulled up short and turned to Zozimo. "How are we going to get there?"

The wizard shrugged. "I knew I was forgetting something."

"Don't you have a transporting spell?"

"That falls under black magic," frowned the white wizard.

"Couldn't you make an exception just this one time—for Indigo?"

"Once the line is crossed, there's no going back."

Ion sighed. "All right. Then we need horses. Follow me."

* * *

The Abaddon throne room had been transformed into a dark vision of gothic romance, though some might think they were preparing for a funeral rather than a wedding—and they might be right.

Dash hovered near the dandified Zimbardo as he surveyed the room. "Anything else you need, Master?"

The sorcerer scanned the room, a hand to his chin. "Hmm…oh yes. I almost forgot. We need an officiant."

"*A what?*" asked Dash.

Zimbardo snapped his fingers at the infuriating fairy. "Someone to marry us, you ignorant flea," he snarled. He clapped his hands, causing a minister's collar to instantly appear around the fairy's neck. With a nod of his head, he sent a black book tumbling through the air in his direction.

Dash caught the book, which was entitled *Marriage Vows*.

"Memorize it—fast!" ordered the sorcerer.

137

Gulping, Dash flipped open the book and began rapidly reading, moving his lips as he did so.

* * *

Ion led Zozimo the short way back to Beringer. While the wizard waited in the trees, so as not to be seen, Ion snuck into the kitchen and snatched up some quick sustenance, including bread, cheese, apples and cold meats.

The kitchen staff greeted him cordially. They were fond of the kind-hearted young prince and paid him little heed as he dropped the food items into a satchel.

Ion was just leaving the kitchen when he was unfortunately confronted by his oldest brother, Boron (who spent a great deal of time in the kitchen).

"There you are, you selfish little coward! Where have you been all this time?" his chubby brother scolded him. "Mother and father have been worried sick about you."

"Sorry," mumbled Ion. "I was away on an urgent errand for Zozimo. There was no time to send word."

He attempted to brush past his brother, but Boron deliberately stepped into his way, blocking the exit with his bulky frame. He eyed the bulging satchel suspiciously. "What's in the bag?"

"Just some old apples and moldy cheese," shrugged Ion. "But I think Cook is preparing a stuffed goose for dinner."

"Really? That's my favorite!" Forgetting to bully his brother, Boron hurried past him into the kitchen, hoping to get some stuffed goose.

Relieved, as he did not want to have to explain himself, Ion quickly exited the kitchen. Zozimo emerged from the trees, and Ion handed him the satchel of food. Then he raced off toward the stables.

Nyx hungrily nosed the bag in the wizard's hand.

Benevolently, Zozimo reached into the bag and drew out a large turkey leg, which he tossed to the wolf, who quickly devoured it. Shrugging, the wizard pulled out an apple for himself and took a big bite.

Ion returned shortly, leading two of their swiftest horses, including his favorite black steed, Lucifer (who had earlier abandoned him). The other was a lordly white stallion named Lightning.

Zozimo eyed the high prancing steeds a bit nervously as he munched his apple. "Spirited, aren't they? It's been a while since I did any riding," he confided.

"Come on, you're a wizard. You should at least be able to ride a horse," chided Ion. "Don't you have a horse riding potion or something?"

The wizard shook his head dismissively. "There's no such thing. I'll just have to take my chances."

"You can ride Lightning," he said, indicating the white horse. "He's not quite as touchy as Lucifer." Tentatively, the wizard approached the tall white steed and patted its nose. "There's a good boy. Take it easy on these old bones."

The horse whinnied and nicked away his apple. "You owe me," the wizard told the horse.

Ion helped the wizard into Lightning's saddle and then quickly swung up onto Lucifer's back. "Let's go!" he shouted. "We've lost enough time. If we ride hard, we should be there by sundown. Hopefully, it won't be too late."

The two horses galloped off into the late afternoon. Zozimo bounced painfully atop the fleet white stallion, which proved to be aptly named. "I'll pay for this tomorrow," he muttered. *If there is a tomorrow*, he thought ruefully.

Several hours later, the riders emerged from the woods on a high hill overlooking the quaint Village of Abaddon. Sunset was already streaking the sky with deep tones of rose, gold, and copper. Quickly, they rode their mounts down the hill into the village. Curiously, no one seemed to be about. When they did encounter some villagers, they appeared to be stuck in the middle of the road. Carefully, they rode around them.

"What's wrong with them?" Ion asked bemused.

"It appears that Zimbardo has placed a sticking spell over the entire kingdom," frowned the wizard. "We'd better hurry."

They rode rapidly through the village to the outskirts of town. There, on a low rising hill before them, loomed the gleaming Castle of Abaddon. The great metal sconces had already been lit for the evening, but there was no other sign of activity. Quietly, they urged on their horses.

* * *

Inside the Abaddon throne room, the Design Demons were flitting about putting the final touches on the black wedding. In his wedding finery, Zimbardo waited impatiently at the top of the room. The raised area adjacent to the two thrones had been turned into a kind of unholy altar complete with a canopy decorated with the unnatural black roses.

Zimbardo raised an arm. "Enough!" he declared to the industrious demons. "Let us begin!'

Excitedly, the demons quickly disposed of their trash and tools. Primping each other, they took front row seats, heedlessly sitting atop the paralyzed spectators, or callously shoving them to the floor to make room for themselves.

At the side of the altar, a ghoulish demon in black tails conducted a demon orchestra complete with strings and brass. At Zimbardo's nod, they struck up a dirge-like parody of *The Wedding March.*

Holding the volume of wedding vows, Dash nervously took his place at the altar next to Zimbardo.

The doors burst open at the other end of the room. Indigo made a grand entrance as she appeared in the doorway adorned in the magnificent black wedding gown. Attended by the Fashion Demons, she appeared to float into the room and up the aisle. Her feet were unchained, but her wrists remain shackled together. Between her silver gauntlets, she clutched a bouquet of blood red roses—much like the bouquet Zimbardo had presented to her mother on her fateful wedding day. The Fashion Demons trailed behind Indigo, holding up her very long, black lace train.

At the top of the room, Zimbardo beamed proudly as his extraordinarily beautiful bride approached him. He had waited a very long time to enjoy the comforts of connubial bliss, but he reflected now that it had been worth the wait.

Indigo proceeded as slowly as possible up the aisle, passing by the immobilized guests and twittering demons. Frantically, she reconsidered her options. She could continue up the aisle and marry the ghastly sorcerer as he demanded—or try to make a last ditch run for it, though the prospect of that seemed unlikely, if not futile. Then she caught sight of her father, who remained slumped against the wall. In passing, she saw the look of horror in his eyes and knew she really had no choice. She must marry Zimbardo or her father would surely die.

Resigned to her dismal fate, Indigo finished the longest walk of her life and reluctantly took her place beside Zimbardo at the altar.

The sorcerer leered at her appreciatively. "You look magnificent!"

"Bite me!" muttered Indigo, refusing to look at him.

"Later..." he promised lewdly.

Indigo shuddered. She thought she might expire of disgust on the spot.

Sensing her lack of enthusiasm, Zimbardo reached into his vest pocket and drew out the bottle containing the cure. "Just say *I do*," he reminded her. He shook the bottle enticingly and then tucked it back into his pocket.

"Let's get this over with," she sighed.

Zimbardo turned to Dash, who really wanted no part of marrying this young girl to his dreadful master. "Begin!" he ordered him.

Reluctantly, Dash cleared his throat. "We are gathered here today to join this man and this woman in unholy matrimony. If anyone here knows any reason why these two..."

"Skip that part!" snapped the sorcerer. "Get to the vows!"

Dash cleared his throat again. So much for stalling. "Do you, Zimbardo, take Princess Indigo to be your wife?"

"I do!" declared the sorcerer in triumphant tones. He turned eagerly to his bride.

Dash continued, "Do you, Princess Indigo, take this deranged man, Zimbardo, to be your husband?"

The sorcerer cast the fairy a warning look but held his tongue as he waited for Indigo's reply.

A long pause ensued as Indigo tried to form the words. "I..."

Before she could finish, the rear chamber doors were bashed open in a timely interruption of the proceedings.

Chapter Twelve

Heroes Always Arrive Late

Ion and Zozimo barged through the chamber doors followed by a growling Nyx and hovering Bijou. "Indigo, don't do it!" shouted Ion as he caught sight of her in the black wedding gown, standing at the altar beside Zimbardo.

Stunned, Indigo whirled around. "Ion!" she cried. She was amazed to see him racing up the aisle followed by Nyx, Zozimo, and Bijou. *Thank heavens they're all right—at least until now*, she reflected grimly. Since her abduction, she had feared the worst.

Growling menacingly, Nyx slunk forward ready to pounce upon the sorcerer, who had taken his mistress.

"No, Nyx, stay back!" she cried in alarm as Zimbardo lifted a threatening arm to him. The wolf froze in his tracks but continued to snarl.

Zimbardo grabbed hold of Indigo and pulled her in front of him, using her as a human shield. "Zozimo!" exclaimed the sorcerer. "It's been a long time, Brother."

142

Ion cast a look of astonishment at the wizard. "*Brother?*"

Zozimo shrugged. "You can't pick your relatives."

"Nice of you to come to my wedding," said the sorcerer. "Sadly, you're not on the guest list, so I suggest you leave now…"

Ion pulled his dagger and stepped forward. "Let her go!"

"Prince Ion, I believe?" the sorcerer inquired.

Ion nodded at him shortly.

"I can see that you care for the girl, but I fear you're too late. She's already agreed to be my wife. Haven't you, Princess?" He smirked as Indigo struggled desperately against him.

"That's not true!" she cried indignantly. "I only said *I.*"

Zimbardo waved his hand dismissively. "A mere technicality. You are mine now. Better luck next time, Prince Ion. Now run along to mommy. "

"Release her at once!" demanded Ion furiously.

Zimbardo laughed mirthlessly. "Come now, this is getting tedious, boy. "You must know I'm just toying with you for my amusement. In another second I 'll lift my hand and freeze you in place like the rest of this feckless court."

Zozimo stepped forward. "I'm afraid not, Zimbardo. I've already placed a protective spell around us, which is impossible to reverse."

"Touché, brother! I see you're getting better in your old age."

Zozimo observed him with a steely glare. "Because we are brothers, I will give you a chance to redeem yourself. Leave the girl and walk away now. Or face the consequences," he warned gravely.

"Ooh, I'm scared." The sorcerer's voice dripped with sarcasm.

"*Hells' bells*, Brother!" scolded the wizard. "If you want a wife, why don't you choose someone your own age?"

"Now where's the fun in *that?*" The sorcerer chuckled wickedly. "Besides, as usual you're missing the point, Brother. Surely, even you can see that Princess Indigo and I are a perfect match."

"What do you mean?" Zozimo frowned at him. As far as he was concerned there couldn't possibly be a worse match.

"Why should I stop at Abaddon, when there are so many other kingdoms to conquer? With Indigo by my side—and her *special touch*— I'll not only have the perfect trophy wife, I'll have the perfect weapon."

With her high-heeled slipper, Indigo stomped on the sorcerer's foot as hard as she possibly could, trying vainly to twist out of his grasp.

"Oww! Take her!" he cried, thrusting Indigo away from him as he hopped on one foot and rubbed the other.

A host of demons immediately leapt forward and seized hold of Indigo. "Don't worry, my love," growled Zimbardo. " This won't take long."

Smiling maliciously, he stepped down from the dais and rolled up his sequin-studded sleeves. "I'm going to enjoy this. After all, every wedding needs a little entertainment."

Grasping his dagger, Ion stepped boldly forward to meet him. "The pleasure will be all mine," he assured the sorcerer, smiling at him with equal menace.

Zozimo stepped protectively in front of Ion to address his brother. "You've sunk even lower than I thought. You were the most gifted of us all, Zimbardo, but you threw it all away when you chose the path of darkness and revenge."

"You're the loser, Brother. I used to look up to you until I realized how pathetic you are. Look at you; you're nothing but a poor peddler in the woods, selling paltry potions to peasants. I, on the other hand, am the most powerful and feared sorcerer in the Five Kingdoms. And, after today, I will have everything I've ever desired."

"Don't do this, I beg you!" the wizard pleaded. Though his brother was now beyond redemption in his eyes, he would take no pleasure in killing him.

"Too late!" Zimbardo raised his arms and released two bolts of burning energy at his brother.

Zozimo easily fended off the attack with his staff, causing the energy bolts to ricochet back toward Zimbardo. The sorcerer repelled the rebound bolts and sent them flying back to his brother.   In a magical standoff, sorcerer and wizard continued to assault each other with potentially lethal energy balls.

Crouched behind the throne, Dash almost got whiplash as he watched the two warring brothers exchanging the ping-pong like energy balls.

Ion attempted to go to Zozimo's aid but was bombarded by attacking demons. He slashed wildly at them with his dagger, causing many of them to shriek and disappear.

Bijou hovered over the battle scene, dropping the potion bombs on the demons. Amazingly, the potion bombs neutralized the demons and turned them into benign butterflies, which flitted harmlessly about the room.

Nyx lunged forward, desperate to reach his mistress but was easily repelled by the half dozen demons, who held her securely in place. "Nyx, watch out!" Indigo cried as the large wolf was sent tumbling across the room.

Dazed, the wolf staggered to his feet and caught sight of Dash, crouching behind the king's throne. Sniffing, he recognized the fairy's scent. Growling, he slunk forward, ready to leap upon the fairy.

Terrified, Dash quickly sprinkled the wolf's snout with fairy dust, instantly disarming him. Gingerly, he patted the confused wolf on the head. "That's a nice wolfie. Run along now."

Shaking his head to clear it, Nyx jumped back into the fray.

Zimbardo and Zozimo remained in a conjuror's standoff as they continued to throw and dodge each other's deadly energy bolts.

Seeing that his master was thus engaged with Zozimo, Dash flew over to Ion, who was still slashing wildly at the dive-bombing demons.

Startled by the fairy, Ion took a swipe at Dash, who backed off in alarm.

"Hey, Kid, I'm on your side," he whispered urgently. "Get Zimbardo's amulet," he pointed to the identical amulet around his own neck. "And I can help you."

Ion frowned at the fairy as he continued to thrust wildly at the bombarding demons. "Why should I trust you?"

"Are you kidding?" cried the beleaguered fairy. "I can't stand Zimbardo. But as long as he's wearing that blasted amulet, I'm stuck with him."

Before he could reply, Ion's attention was distracted by a fresh horde of attacking demons.

Sighing, Dash retreated to his hiding place behind the throne. At this rate, he feared things would not end well for anyone—except Zimbardo.

The brothers continued to hurl larger and larger energy bolts at each other, but neither seemed able to harm the other.

"Time out, Brother!" the sorcerer threw up his hands as though conceding the battle.

Warily, Zozimo stayed his arm.

"You've got more fight in you than I thought," said the sorcerer, breathing a bit heavily. "But I'm getting tired of playing games with you."

Catching his brother off guard, Zimbardo unleashed a huge blast of dark energy, which crackled loudly around Zozimo, sending up sparks and smoke. The dark energy was so potent that it was able to penetrate the protective spell around the wizard. Zozimo's entire body seemed to light up from the inside as he shook uncontrollably. Abruptly, he fell to the ground, unconscious.

Ion saw the wizard fall and dashed to his side. "Zozimo!" He shook the stricken wizard but he remained ominously still.

Enraged, Ion drew his dagger and charged toward the sorcerer.

Zimbardo held up a warning arm. "Don't even try it. There's more where that came from," he snarled.

Undaunted, Ion flung himself at the black magician.

At that moment, Bijou dive-bombed Zimbardo, circling his head and furiously pummeling his face with his feet.

While the sorcerer was distracted by Bijou, Ion managed to cut off his amulet with his dagger and drop it into his pocket.

Unaware of his missing amulet, Zimbardo cast off Bijou with another blast of dark energy, which sent the bat hurtling into the rafters. Stunned, he swung upside down, trying to catch his breath.

The bat had managed to inflict a fair amount of damage on Zimbardo's no longer so pretty face. As the sorcerer moaned and clutched his bleeding nose, Ion once again leapt at him, brandishing his dagger.

Zimbardo tried to dodge the blow but sustained a slash to his chin. Gasping, he put a hand to his bleeding jaw. "Now I'm really mad," he growled. "You've gone and ruined my wedding portrait."

Infuriated, the sorcerer directed a tazer-like bolt at Ion. The impact caused his dagger to clatter to the floor and sent him flying across the room.

Zimbardo stalked across the room to where Ion lay and planted a booted foot upon his heaving chest. "You pathetic boy, did you really think you could have the princess? You're way out of your league, and now it's time to permanently bench you."

"Let him go!" cried Indigo.   She could not bear it if she were the cause of Ion's death.

"I cannot!" snapped the testy sorcerer.

"Why not?" she demanded.

"Do you think me blind?" he growled at her.   "It's as plain as a wart on a witch's nose.   The boy is in love with you, so he must die."

Under Zimbardo's boot, Ion blinked up at the sorcerer in surprise. It's true, he realized. He *was* in love with Indigo!

"If you hurt him," she said. "I will refuse to marry you. Let him live, and we'll finish the ceremony."

Zimbardo considered.   Clearly, it was better to trick her into cooperation and finish the boy later. "Very well…" He turned to Ion, "Get lost!" He directed a second, tazer-like bolt at Ion, launching him further across the room where he appeared to lie unconscious.

Growling, Nyx launched himself at Zimbardo's throat. "You, too!" cried Zimbardo as he tazered the wolf, sending him airborne as well. The wolf hurtled up against Ion's unmoving body and lay equally inert beside him.

Gathering himself, Zimbardo crossed back to the altar where Indigo struggled futilely in the grasp of the Fashion Demons. "Don't worry, my sweet, " he assured her. "They're just *napping.*"   He put a hand to his bloodied chin and winced. "Oh dear, I'm still bleeding." He turned back to Indigo. "Forgive me a moment. I want this to be perfect."

He stepped away from the altar and motioned to the Fashion Demons. "Make-up!"

Taking charge, Dash moved forward assertively and grabbed hold of Indigo's arm. "Don't worry, Master, I've got her." He shooed away the Fashion Demons who were clutching her. "Run along…"

The Fashion Demons released Indigo to Dash and rushed forward to attend to Zimbardo's battered face.

While Zimbardo's back was turned, Dash put a finger to his lips, motioning Indigo to remain quiet. Making sure no one else could see, he quickly sprinkled her chained wrists with fairy dust, causing the locks to spring open softly, though the chains remained in place.   Astonished, Indigo nodded her thanks to the fairy.

Innocently, Dash resumed his place as wedding officiant, clearing his throat and straightening his clothes.

With his make-up heavily retouched, Zimbardo rejoined Indigo at the altar. "Now, where were we before we were so rudely interrupted? Oh, yes, I think you were about to become my wife." He motioned to Dash. "Repeat that last question, please."

The fairy cleared his throat again, exchanging covert glances with Indigo. "Do you, Princess Indigo, take this so-called man to be your unlawfully wedded husband?"

Zimbardo looked askance at the impertinent fairy. There would be plenty of time to deal with him later…

All eyes (except, of course, the ones that couldn't move) once again turned expectantly to Indigo, waiting for her reply.

Indigo shuddered as she considered her prospective groom. The thick white make up had been liberally plastered over his bruised face, causing him to look like a pasty-faced ghoul. She could just see the tip of the bottle containing her stolen cure, peeking out from his vest pocket.

Zimbardo leered at her impatiently. "Come now, my love, don't keep me in any further suspense. What say you?"

There was a strange, unexpected clanking sound.

"I say go to hell!" Indigo shouted boldly. Unexpectedly, she lunged forward, thrusting her large blood red bouquet into Zimbardo's face. At the same time, she reached with her other hand for the bottled cure inside the sorcerer's vest pocket.

Zimbardo's hand immediately shot up, grabbing Indigo's hand around the wrist before she could reach the bottle.   He spat out the dark red petals filling his mouth. "Not so…f…fast!" he choked.

Belatedly, Zimbardo realized that he was clutching Indigo's bare, discolored hand! "Nooo!" he cried in abject terror, instantly dropping her hand.   But it was too late. He glanced down and saw that both her hand shackles and silver gauntlets were now lying on the floor at his feet.

"How?" he gasped in astonishment.

Dash darted forward and waved smugly at the stricken sorcerer.

"You!" Zimbardo felt for the amulet that was always around his neck, intending to permanently incinerate the fairy. Shocked, he realized it was missing. The hand that had grasped Indigo's wrist was already beginning to burn and tingle. Crazed with fear and rage, he lunged blindly at Dash, who easily eluded his grasp.

Mesmerized with shock, Indigo stared as Zimbardo's hand rapidly began to blacken with rot.

With his other hand, the howling sorcerer attempted to grab the cure from his vest pocket. Weakly, he clutched the bottle, waving it at Indigo. "Thanks for this," he sneered.

Before Zimbardo could pull the stopper from the bottle with his teeth and drink the contents, Dash swooped back in and snatched the bottle from his master's withering hand. "I'll take that!"

With a bloodcurdling screech, Zimbardo crumpled to the floor, writhing in agony as the corruption coursed rapidly through his body.   He glared up vengefully at the defiant princess. "If I can't have you, no one will!" he croaked. With a final, dying effort, he raised his hand and directed a lethal blast of dark energy at her.

Stunned, Indigo's eyes fell shut and all color drained from her face. She dropped to the floor next to Zimbardo and lay beside him, as still as a corpse.

Grimly satisfied, the dying sorcerer turned his head to regard Indigo's lifeless form. *"I...win,"* he croaked with his last breath.

Zimbardo's body convulsed violently as the deadly affliction literally ate him up from the inside out. The virulent rot spread over his once handsome face, until the gruesome black goo began to seep from his eyes, nose, and mouth.

Ding dong, the wicked sorcerer was finally dead—killed by his own curse!

Demon arms appeared, rising up through the ground and dragged down the grotesque remains of Zimbardo's corpse.

Dash watched with satisfaction as his cruel master was drawn away. "Bon voyage, hope you enjoy your honeymoon in hell."

With Zimbardo's death, the paralyzed people in the throne room (and throughout the kingdom) were relieved of his dreadful sticking spell and began to move about in a daze. The room rapidly filled with chaos as everyone began to chatter at once about the horrific events, which had transpired before their transfixed eyes.

Lying beside each other, Ion and Nyx opened their eyes and staggered to their feet. Horrified, they spied Indigo's inert form sprawled upon the floor. *Indigo!* Together, they rushed to the side of the fallen princess.

Ion knelt beside her and cradled her lifeless form in his arms. "Oh no, no! Not this! Indigo, wake up, please wake up!" He shook her, trying vainly to wake her.

Beside him, Nyx sniffed at her and licked her face, trying desperately to wake his mistress, but her eyes remained resolutely closed. The forlorn wolf whimpered and then howled his grief.

Clutching the bottled cure, Dash flew over to Ion and tapped him on the shoulder. "Hey, kid, try this…"

Raising his head, Ion blinked in surprise at the familiar bottle in Dash's hand. "Is that…?"

The fairy nodded.

Uncertainly, Ion took the bottle from the fairy and carefully removed the stopper. Lifting Indigo's head, he poured the entire contents down her throat. He waited expectantly for her eyes to open. But they did not. She remained lifeless and unmoving in his arms.

Bending over her, Ion began to grieve. "This can't be! Was it all for nothing?"

Beside him, Nyx shared his grief, howling mournfully.

Laying Indigo gently on the ground, Ion turned and wrapped his arms around the howling wolf, burying his face in his fur.

While they grieved together, Indigo's entire body began to glow with a white light. The discoloration of her hands began to gradually disappear. Slowly, Indigo opened her eyes and sat up, observing the grieving boy and wolf.

"What happened?" she asked in confusion.

Ion and Nyx lifted their heads, stunned to see her looking at them. "You're alive!" cried Ion.

Then he glanced down. "Indigo, your hands!"

Indigo raised her now perfect hands, studying them incredulously. "They're normal! Ion, they're normal!"

Jubilant, he attempted to reach for her hands. Reflexively, she pulled them away.

Again, Ion intentionally reached for her hands. This time, she didn't pull away.

Indigo tensed worriedly, staring at Ion's hands, waiting for them to turn black and start rotting. But there was no change. His hands remained perfect.

He smiled at her. "You're cured!"

"How?" she asked perplexed.

Ion held up the potion bottle, turning it over to show that it was empty.

"How did you get it from Zimbardo?" she gasped.

"It's a long story. I'll tell you later," he smiled at her, continuing to hold her hands in his.

Indigo glanced around anxiously. "Where is he?"

"Zimbardo?" asked Ion.

She nodded. "The last thing I remember I was trying to get the cure from his pocket, but he grabbed my hand. . .is he. . .?"

Ion nodded. "He won't be cursing anyone ever again."

"So...I...?" she broke off, unable to say the words.

Ion nodded again. "You did."

"Good!" Indigo exulted. A gratified smile spread slowly over her face. The world was simply better off without some people, especially villainous sorcerers!

Ion pulled her to her feet and, holding hands, they began to spin giddily around the room. Unexpectedly, Ion suddenly stopped whirling and pulled Indigo into his arms. Staring into those phenomenal purple blue eyes, he bent his head to hers, and, at long last, pressed his mouth to those luscious red lips.

As fairies don't have the best timing, Dash flew over at that moment and tapped Ion on the shoulder, interrupting their first kiss.

Reluctantly, they broke their embrace and turned to face the fairy.

"Hey, nice work, you kids. Thanks for offing the Evil One. I'm finally free."

"We couldn't have done it without your help," said Ion gratefully.

"How can we repay you?" asked Indigo, smiling at the impish fairy.

"Could I have the amulet?" asked Dash.

Ion had forgotten he had the sorcerer's amulet. Feeling in his pocket, he drew it out and handed it to the fairy. "I trust you'll use it wisely?"

The fairy nodded as he tucked away the amulet into his robe. "Thanks, I owe you a fairy favor. Just ask for Dash." He turned away, poised to fly off then paused. "Oh…and good luck with the relationship thing." Saluting them, he flew off through the window.

Feeling a little forgotten, Nyx nosed his way between the happy couple, growling a little jealously at Ion.

Indigo crouched down to embrace the beautiful silver wolf. "Don't worry, Nyx. I love you, too." As she hugged the wolf, her eyes met Ion's and they smiled dreamily at each other.

From sheer happiness, Ion drew Indigo back up to her feet and they continued to hold hands and whirl about the room. Wanting to be included, Nyx barked and leapt up playfully between the joyously spinning couple.

Because his protective spell had not been entirely eliminated, Zozimo was only slightly singed from Zimbardo's energy bolts. Groggily, he regained his feet and stood with Bijou perched upon his shoulder. Both looked on in satisfaction as they watched Ion and Indigo twirling jubilantly about the room.

"We did it!" the wizard exclaimed joyfully. He turned to his small but able assistant. "Good job, my friend."

Bijou nodded in acknowledgement. After all, if he had not followed Indigo when she had been abducted, and warned Zozimo of his brother's evil machinations, and pummeled the sorcerer's face with his feet, Zimbardo would doubtless still be alive, and Indigo would probably be Mrs. Zimbardo by now. The bat puffed his small chest out, proudly. The wingless ones could be so clueless sometimes.

Spotting King Azrael still slumped against the wall, Zozimo hurried over and helped him to his feet. "Your Highness, are you all right?"

"Yes, yes, I'm fine but what of Indigo?" he asked urgently.

"Look for yourself," said the wizard.

Gazing across the room, King Azrael was amazed to see his daughter in the embrace of a handsome young man. "Indigo!" he cried in astonishment.

Hearing her father, Indigo broke from Ion's arms and raced over to him, waving her unblemished hands. "Father, look! The curse is gone!"

"At last!" he exclaimed.   Jubilantly, he embraced his daughter. "Your mother would be so happy."

Ion approached the pair a bit tentatively and stood smiling behind Indigo.

The king regarded him closely. "So…who is this?"

Indigo turned to smile at Ion and took his hand. "Father, I'd like you to meet Prince Ion of Beringer."

Ion bowed low to the king. "Your Majesty."

"Prince, is it?" asked the king.

Ion nodded.

"What took you so long?" he asked, only half-teasing.

The king beamed his approval at the young couple as they exchanged bashful glances.

Epilogue

News of Zimbardo's death spread rapidly throughout the Five Kingdoms and was met with much relief and celebration. Crystal Repair men (and women) could once more practice their trade without fear of death and retribution. After a long period of sadness and despair, the Kingdom of Abaddon was once more alive with happiness and celebration. After knowing each other for just two weeks, Ion had gotten down on one knee and proposed marriage to Princess Indigo. Though she had never planned to marry so young, she knew he was *the one*, so she said *yes,* and he slipped the largest diamond and sapphire ring onto her finger that had ever been seen in the Five Kingdoms.

King Azrael was so overjoyed at his daughter's betrothal to Prince Ion that he decided to host another gala ball, this time to celebrate her engagement.

Light streamed from every window in the castle as a long line of fashionably dressed guests poured through the open doors. Everyone was eager to make the acquaintance of the young couple and to hear firsthand the account of their fabled adventures. While Indigo's debut ball had been an extremely tense and sorry affair, the couple's engagement ball would be remembered for years to come as the most extravagant and entertaining ball to ever take place in the Five Kingdoms.

Once again, King Azrael had spared no expense in overseeing the celebration feast.   Long tables stretched across the hall laden with heaping platters of the finest foods and delicacies.   The royal orchestra played the very latest waltz tunes, and the ballroom floor spilled over with gaily twirling couples.

In the reception line, Princess Indigo and Prince Ion stood beaming, arm-in-arm, beside King Azrael, greeting the guests as they arrived. The princess was a vision in a flowing gown of sparkling silver and sapphire blue, which exactly matched her magnificent engagement ring.   Of course, she also wore her mother's sparkling earrings, which had somehow survived her ordeal.

Beside her, Ion looked very dashing in the royal blue dress uniform of Beringer.   It was a good thing he was already engaged, because quite a few of the young ladies in attendance cast more than a few wistful looks in his direction. How had they not noticed him before? Similarly, the young men of the kingdom were kicking themselves for having overlooked the enchanting Princess Indigo. What fools they had been to let something like a little curse stop them from pursuing her!

Nyx was no longer banished from the ballroom. The silver wolf sat attentively at Indigo's feet and looked quite regal due to the Royal Medallion of Bravery, which had been draped around his neck in recognition of his devoted service to the princess.   It was, however, quite hard for the hungry wolf to ignore all the delectable foods that were laid out so temptingly before him.

As a servant passed by with a stack full of discarded plates, Indigo discreetly snatched away a still meaty bone and slipped it to her faithful companion.   "Good boy, Nyx, you deserve this." She patted the wolf as he happily settled down at her feet to gnaw the delectable bone.

King Azrael was surprised to find himself surrounded by quite a number of matronly single ladies. While he enjoyed their attentions and danced with quite a few, his eyes returned repeatedly to the large portrait of his late queen, Citrine, which hung in the ballroom. Was it just his imagination, or did she seem to be smiling at him?

Though Zozimo could not remember when he had last attended a ball, he had made an exception for Ion and Indigo's engagement and had donned his best wizard's gown for the occasion, even trimming his hair and beard so that he actually looked almost handsome. Still, he stood a bit awkwardly at the side of the dance floor, not quite sure what to do at such a splendid event.

Bijou accompanied his master and perched on the wizard's shoulder, trying not to frighten the guests, who had never before seen an invited bat at a royal ball. He smiled and waved affably to the surprised dancers, while Zozimo assured everyone who inquired that the bat was quite knowledgeable and well behaved and carried no infectious diseases.

Abigail had taken unusual pains with her appearance and looked quite lovely in a rose-colored gown. She was slightly acquainted with Zozimo, as it had been she who had always visited him to place the orders for Indigo's gauntlets. Previously, she had regarded him as a rather crotchety, if wise, old man. However, cleaned up in his white wizard's robe, he looked downright appealing.

Catching his eye, Abigail smiled at the wizard, causing his cheeks to flame as pink as her dress. Boldly, she approached him and, with some persuasion, managed to pull the reluctant wizard onto the dance floor.

Having lost his perch on the wizard's shoulder, Bijou flew up into the ballroom rafters where he was much more comfortable and dined on some of the tasty royal insects, that lived there in unsuspected abundance.

Ion's parents, the King and Queen of Beringer, were also present and stood proudly in the reception line next to King Azrael. They were very happy to see their youngest—and wildest—son, Ion, so well matched to the kind and lovely young Princess Indigo. Now they only had to worry about their *other* six sons, and they were indeed quite worrisome. While all six of them were in attendance, they seemed to have forgotten that they had earlier passed up their chance with the young princess at her debut ball. They looked on jealously as Ion whizzed by in the arms of his exquisite fiancée.

"How come he gets the girl? Boron complained bitterly. His brothers shrugged, completely at a loss, as each secretly considered himself to be *the best* Beringer brother.

Hugely annoyed, Boron cast about among the other young women attending the ball, searching for someone who even came close to the young princess, but they already seemed to be occupied with someone else. He was just about to give up his search for a suitable partner and visit the buffet table for the third time, when he beheld the ugliest woman he had even seen making a beeline toward him.

In fact, the heavyset, ugly woman was the same one who had earlier ordered the love potion from Ion. So far, she had not had any luck in finding a suitor, but, upon spying the chubby Boron, she thought him to be the most handsome man she had ever seen. Clutching the potion to her chest, she chased him across the dance floor and out onto the veranda. Cornered, Boron was forced to politely accept the bottle she offered him. Seeing that it was actually full of whiskey, he drank quite a lot of it until he began to think the woman was not so ugly after all...

Dash was not present at the ball but went on to make a fortune by going on the lecture circuit. He was widely in demand throughout the Five Kingdoms of the mortals, as well as the Twenty Kingdoms of the fairies. He gave quite an excellent impersonation of the late, unlamented sorcerer and both horrified and amused his listeners with his only slightly embellished accounts of Zimbardo's evil deeds and vainglorious foibles.

Gazing adoringly into each other's eyes, Indigo and Ion continued to whirl blissfully around the dance floor oblivious of the fact that all eyes were upon them, this time with admiration rather than suspicion.

The same old ladies, who had earlier disparaged Indigo as a *witch* at her debut ball, now saw her quite differently.

"She's so sweet," cooed the first grand dame. "I never believed all those terrible things they said about her."

Her elder friend nodded in agreement. "Her eyes are too beautiful to be evil."

The young couple overheard the remarks as they swept by the old women and chuckled at the irony.

"It seems I no longer inspire fear," said Indigo.

"That's not true," the prince replied, gazing into her fabulous indigo eyes. "I greatly fear that I am not worthy of you, and that I will not be able to give you all the happiness you deserve."

"Don't worry. You already have," she assured him with a loving smile.

Cured of her deadly curse, Princess Indigo went on to become a great favorite throughout the Five Kingdoms and was widely revered for the great courage she had shown in dispatching the nefarious sorcerer who had abducted her and then tried to turn her into his evil bride.

As a natural healer, Indigo decided to continue her research experiments in the greenhouse and nobly attempted to find a cure for the plague. Although she was not successful in this, she did discover a cure for *dragon bumps,* the odious affliction, which had taken the lives of her grandparents. In fact, it was so thoroughly eradicated in her time that it was never again reported.

Prince Ion was also highly regarded, both for his blond good looks, and for the gallant role he had played in helping Indigo find her cure and destroy the dastardly Zimbardo. Zozimo was so favorably impressed by the courageous actions of his young protégé that he promoted him to Apothecary First Class.

The popular royal pair became known as the *it couple* of their day, often referred to as *"I-I"* (or *"aye-aye")*. Indeed, it was hard to pick up a local parchment without reading another story about the golden couple. Together, they went on to raise quite a few charming, if often troublesome, young princes and princesses. Fairly often, there were unsubstantiated reports of various scandals and affairs rocking the royal court, but, as real couples do, they lived, more or less, happily ever after.

The End

Acknowledgement

The first draft of Princess Death was written while Shaina was away at college. We collaborated on an almost daily basis over Skype, which, to say the least, was a frustrating and challenging process due to the many technical "glitches" we encountered. However, even that gave rise to inspiration for our sorcerer villain, Zimbardo. We want to acknowledge the mutual persistence, dedication, and creative collaboration that went into writing and completing our first novel-it wasn't easy-but it was fun! We want to thank our host of beta readers along the way, who were an invaluable aid in shaping our final story. In particular, we want to thank our brother/uncle, Michael, for his astute, articulate, and enthusiastic analysis and support. Our beautiful late cat, Lainie, served as our feline muse during the writing of Princess Death and is sorely missed. Currently, feline muse duties have been taken over by our very clever and handsome silver cat, Mr. Nyx, who was, of course, named after Princes Indigo's faithful silver wolf companion, Nyx. Much appreciation and thanks to our good friend and exceptional, eagle-eyed editor, Kathleen Cole, who has a lot of post-its and a classical distaste for the overuse of italics and exclamation points. (Sorry, Kathleen!) Kudos to our wonderful cover designer, Donna Collier of DLC Designs, who so perfectly executed our murky vision and gave us such a stunning cover. Thank you, as well, to Alec McKinley, who provided us with an excellent and cartographically correct fantasy map of The Five Kingdoms. Lastly and always, we have to thank our incredibly supportive, smart, and accomplished husband/father, Ivan, for his expert legal and technical know-how and guidance, which makes it possible for two techno-phobes to succeed. If you are reading this, thank you, too!

ABOUT THE AUTHORS

JEANNE GRANDILLI and SHAINA ROTHBERG

Jeanne Grandilli and Shaina Rothberg are a mother-daughter writing team and the co-publishers of Bon Bon Books. *Princess Death, Tale of a Cursed Princess* is their first novel, though they plan to write many others in a variety of genres. Previously, Jeanne worked in the Hollywood film industry as a studio story analyst, including 15 years at Disney Pictures. Before turning to novel writing, she penned numerous optioned screenplays and two stage plays, many in collaboration with her husband, Ivan Rothberg. She attended UCLA where she received a BA in English and an MFA in Film/Screenwriting. Shaina is a trained artist and prolific storyteller. She is a graduate of Chapman University and holds a BA degree in Digital Arts with a specialization in Animation and Art Direction. They live in Los Angeles, California.

BONUS CONTENT

We hope you enjoyed reading the story of *Princess Death, Tale of a Cursed Princess.* As a thank you, we would like to send you a bonus short story about the meeting of Princess Indigo and her beloved wolf companion, Nyx. To receive the free bonus story, "Indigo to the Rescue," visit our website at bonbonbooks.org and click on the link to join our newsletter, *The Bon Mot.*

CONNECT WITH US ONLINE

 bonbonbooks.org

 @bonbonbooksig

 @bonbonbooks

We'd Love to Hear From You!

Thank you so much for reading our book—it means the world to us! If you enjoyed it and thinks others would, as well, would you please take a moment to leave a review? Your feedback not only helps others but also keeps us motivated to create more valuable content for you.

Here's how you can leave a review:

1. Scan the QR code on this page to go directly to the review page.

2. Or, visit your Amazon Orders' page, find this book, and click "Write a Product Review."

Your kind words make a big difference.

Thank you for your support!

www.ingramcontent.com/pod-product-compliance
Lightning Source LLC
Chambersburg PA
CBHW050944120626
46552CB00001B/379